"Larry, what is it? What's wrong?"

We were all staring, the room silent except for her voice. His head was bowed and I couldn't see his face because of the angle, but I heard a dull thud and numbly watched a glass roll across the rug and come to rest against Innis's shoe.

I felt very chilled as I watched Trey cross the room and bend over the love seat. He tilted Lawrence's head back against the cushion, and we could all see the slack face that was a peculiar color, and the half-opened eyes. I don't suppose Trey had to check the carotid pulse, but he did, a frown pulling at his brows, and then looked across the room straight at me and shook his head slightly.

As if from a great distance, I heard Innis speak in a hoarse voice. "We should call a doctor."

"No," Trey said quietly. "We should call the police."

Other Mysteries Featuring
Lane Montana by
Kay Hooper
from Avon Books

CRIME OF PASSION

KAY HOOPER

AVON BOOKS NEW YORK

HOUSE OF CARDS is an original publication of Avon Books. This work has never before appeared in book form. This work is a novel. Any similarity to actual persons or events is purely coincidental.

AVON BOOKS
A division of
The Hearst Corporation
1350 Avenue of the Americas
New York, New York 10019

Copyright © 1991 by Kay Hooper
Published by arrangement with the author
Library of Congress Catalog Card Number: 91-92051
ISBN: 0-380-76198-X

First Avon Books Printing: November 1991

AVON TRADEMARK REG. U.S. PAT. OFF. AND IN OTHER COUNTRIES, MARCA REGISTRADA, HECHO EN U.S.A.

Printed in the U.S.A.

RA 10 9 8 7 6 5 4 3 2 1

ONE

"GOD," Trey said.

From the back seat of the Mercedes, Choo contributed his feelings in the eerily human howl peculiar to Siamese cats. He was in his carrier, and had complained bitterly about it all the way from my loft.

I gave my human companion a wry look of understanding. "Awful, isn't it? My great-grandfather made a trip to Europe, and came home with his head stuffed full of ideas. Behold the result."

It was a stormy Friday afternoon, and not exactly the greatest weather in which to view the ancestral home—even for me, and I knew how the place looked at its best. Trey, poor man, was coming upon it unwarned. My fault, but I had good reason; there are some things which are simply beyond explanation—at least until they're squarely in front of you.

Trey had slowed the car to a crawl, probably to get a good look at the scope of the place rather than from any need for caution, since the long driveway was in good repair.

The whole estate was, in fact. Now, at least. When my parents were married more than thirty years before, the grounds had been a mess and the house, though structurally sound, had been badly in need of renovations. My great-grandfather had spent his last dime on his creation; after that, he'd lived in gradually decaying grandeur and struggled to put food on the table.

I'd never understood why Mother felt compelled not only to keep the house, but also to drop a fortune for maintenance despite the fact that she usually spent no more than a few weeks a year in residence (she loved traveling). It *was* her house; Grandfather left it to Mother unconditionally, with only a mild request that it eventually go to Jason and me, but she could have sold it. Neither my brother nor I would have objected.

Odd, isn't it? That she kept the house, I mean. Other than Jase and me, the house was the only thing remaining of Mother's first marriage, and I would have thought she'd dislike the reminder. I know I would have. I had never asked her about it, though I wondered then if I should. I wondered if I *could*. We'd never talked about important things, Mother and I. My visits "home" had been extremely infrequent and fairly reluctant during the previous ten years or so.

I might not have been there that weekend, except that Mother had cheated. She'd called Trey (I was wild to find out how she'd known about him; I sure as hell hadn't told her) and invited him to accompany me home for the weekend and meet her new husband. Since I'd neglected to warn Trey that I didn't want to go (and had, in fact, already politely turned down the invitation), he'd accepted. After that, I was sort of boxed in.

Which was why my (relatively new) lover and I were about to spend a spring weekend in the company of my family. And why we were both gazing at a house which really did defy explanation.

It wasn't only the gray weather that made the place look gloomy and peculiar. It was built of gray stone, massive amounts of it, and if it hadn't been located in the Deep South, the winter heating bills would have broken the treasury of a small nation. It was, however, nice and cool in summer.

All right, I'm stalling, I admit it. My ancestral home did not look as though it belonged to anyone named Montana. In fact, it didn't look as if it belonged in America, let alone Georgia. To be perfectly honest, it missed being described as a castle only because it had no moat or turrets, and it was on the small side (for a castle). Think of the result if a fairly rich and not too bright American was kidnapped and brainwashed by a mad Austrian prince, then was commanded to go forth and build.

If the house hadn't been set so far back from the road (and from a secondary road at that) and encircled by dense trees, we'd have had tourists taking snapshots like crazy.

Okay, I believe I've made my feelings clear. But I should add that beneath my embarrassment lurked a kind of cockeyed pride and a certain amount of sentimentality. Whatever else it was, the house my great-grandfather had dubbed Gestern (which means "yesterday") was a whimsical, one-of-a-kind, and somewhat arrogant monument to the past. (Just *whose* past I have long pondered and studiously shied away from exploring.)

It wasn't quite so vast as monuments tend to be, I'll say that for Great-Grandfather. And I'll always be grateful he didn't succumb to the lure of a moat.

Anyway. It sat four-square with man-size gargoyles (I swear) perched on each corner of the roof, which was of red slate. The Palladian windows looked a mite peculiar, especially set cheek-by-jowl with a number of the regular square variety, and the life-size stone lions flanking the dozen steps up to the front door had been known to petrify people coming upon them unawares in the dark, but at least there weren't any turrets. Great-Grandfather had come close to a drawbridge, though; the lions wore thick stone collars, which were chained (with massive iron links) to the elaborate stonework on either side of the huge front door.

It looked very old, but actually had been built just before the turn of the century. *This* century. So it was old as houses went, but castles in Europe would sneer.

"Which great-grandfather?" Trey asked absently.

"Paternal." He sent me a glance, but I didn't elaborate. He hadn't asked about my family specifically, and I hadn't volunteered. When he did, I would.

He did.

"Montana isn't a southern name, is it?"

"No, it's the name of a western state. Seriously," I added as he glanced at me again. "The way I heard it, my great-great-grandfather's name was something else when he arrived on these shores—from God knows which country. Incredible as it sounds, no records survive of what that name may have been. Or why he decided to change it. He called himself Joseph Montana, and nobody stepped forward to call him a liar. He settled somewhere up North, had one son, and retired—from whatever business he was engaged in—reasonably wealthy. His son built on the wealth, but chose to settle in California, where he married and also had one son, my grandfather. For some inexplicable reason, Great-Grandfather later transplanted his wife and son to the

South, where he bought one of the surviving plantation homes.''

Trey had parked the Mercedes near the foot of the wide steps, and was listening intently. When I halted, he nodded toward the looming gray stone. ''And this?''

I shrugged. ''Like I said. He took a trip to Europe, came home, and built it. It took every penny he had and cost him his wife as well; she left him and their son, running off with the man who'd bought the old plantation from her husband.''

''Colorful,'' Trey murmured.

''To hear Grandfather tell it, that's a mild word for what went on. The plantation owner sold out, and Grandfather said he never heard from his mother again. When Grandfather died, he left the house and property to my mother and requested that it go—eventually—to Jase and me. He left the two of us a few stock shares and bonds he'd managed to squirrel away, and they ended up doing pretty well the last ten years or so.'' Before Trey could ask another question (the logical one, about where my father had been during all of this), I hastily said, ''Mother's family, on the other hand, is southern to the bone. They're the ones you'll be meeting.''

''None of your father's relatives?''

I smiled brightly. ''I don't have any relatives on my father's side.'' Then I opened the car door and got out.

It wasn't that I was trying to avoid the subject of my father. Well, maybe it was. All right, of *course* it was! There are some things you have a hard time dealing with even after twenty years, and dear old Dad was one of mine. Anyway, I didn't want to talk anymore about the Montana branch of the family; as far as I was concerned, they were all enigmas anyway.

Another enigma was standing on the bottom step between the heads of the two lions. He was of medium height and build, possibly in his late fifties or early sixties, although he still had all his hair and none of it was gray, and he was soberly attired in black.

Alexander was not your usual butler. He was, in fact, Mother's general factotum, majordomo—or any other word you might use to define the hub of her peculiar wheel. Jase and I would have worried a lot more about Mother's globe-trotting if Alexander hadn't been with her. He'd been with her since her first marriage—to our father.

"It's good to see you again, Miss Lane."

I'd protested that form of address in my teens, but had long since given up. "It's good to see you, Alexander. I'm glad Mother hasn't traded you away for some bauble."

That earned a faint smile. Strange as it sounds, Mother had once, years ago, very nearly traded Alexander for a jade bracelet. She couldn't speak the language of the country (I forget which one), and the shopkeeper was in desperate need of a new status symbol, and—well, let's just say it was a narrow escape.

Trey came around the car to join me, and I introduced him to Alexander. After they'd made the proper noises, I added, "Jason isn't here yet, is he?" I hadn't seen his car.

Alexander shook his head. "He called to say he'd be delayed, but I imagine he'll be along soon."

I nodded. "Where have you put us?"

"In Anne's room. I'll have your bags sent up." He turned his head slightly, the way somebody will when they hear something behind them (I didn't hear a thing but that wasn't surprising; Alexander had the ears of a bat), then added, "Excuse me," and went back up the steps into the house.

"Who is—or was—Anne?" Trey wanted to know as I was getting Choo's carrier from the back seat.

"I have no idea, really. All the bedroom suites are named after females—most of them queens. Another of Great-Grandfather's whimsical touches." I pointed up toward the massive gray facade rising above us. "It's there. We get a Palladian window and a dandy view of the driveway."

Was I being sarcastic? Well, a little. I get that way when I'm feeling threatened. And I hadn't realized, until then, just how threatened I felt being there. Old T. Wolfe was right, but he put it wrong, if you ask me. You *can* go home—but for some of us it's not a good idea.

Trey leaned against the car and eyed me for a moment in silence. He'd probably caught the sarcasm—he was quick, and I wasn't what you'd call an expert at hiding my feelings—but he didn't question or comment on it. "Montana, why didn't you warn me?" he asked a bit ruefully.

He almost always calls me by my last name. One of these days, I'm going to ask him why. "You wouldn't have believed me," I said with perfect truth.

After another glance at the house, he accepted that. "Maybe not," he murmured. "This is the most improbable place."

I gripped Choo's carrier and turned to face the house. "Brace yourself," I advised.

"Why?" he asked, accompanying me as I trod resolutely up the wide steps.

"Because Great-Grandfather didn't just bring half-baked ideas back from Europe—he brought all kinds of things. And most of them have survived the years. Wait till you see the bed in Anne's room.'' I half expected him to make some remark (during the past couple of months I'd discovered he had quite a sense of humor, especially about some things), but the first glimpse of the interior of the house probably deprived him of all ability to speak. It usually did that to people.

We stepped into the entrance hall, which had roughly a quarter acre of polished marble floor and played host to the stairway and a number of doors but hardly any furniture. It didn't need furniture. The heavily carved walls (white paneling) showed more baroque influence and kept you staring too much to notice there was no place to sit. The only circular room in the house, it was open all the way to the heavy dark rafters three floors above, from which hung an immense chandelier.

''Marry me,'' Trey said.

Putting Choo's carrier on the floor and kneeling to free him from bondage, I said dryly, ''This house has the strangest effect on people.''

''I believe that was a no.'' Trey offered me a hand up, grinning faintly, and we both watched as Choo stepped regally from his carrier and marched across the hall, tail high and claws clicking briskly against the marble. ''Where's he going?'' Trey asked.

''The kitchen. Mother's cook spoils him rotten. Choo puts on airs when he's here, so don't expect him to drape himself around your neck the way he does at the loft.''

''I'm crushed.'' Trey looked around the hall once more with real interest. ''Do I get the nickel tour?''

''How's your stamina?''

''You should know.''

''I thought I was your inspiration for feats beyond

most mortals,'' I remarked, wondering with real interest of my own if Anne's bed would provide even more of a stimulus than I could lay claim to.

"You are,'' Trey said. "Lead on.''

He was still holding my hand, and I didn't object. Obediently, I led the way.

JUST FOR THE record, I'd like to explain that I am not wealthy. Investigators who specialize in finding things don't make much money. As I had told Trey, Great-Grandfather had gone broke building the house, and Grandfather hadn't managed to do more than struggle. As for my father . . . never mind. The truth is, until Mother had married for the second time when I was thirteen, there was no money at all beyond what was necessary. After that, things got better. Jase and I had lived—mostly—in the house with Grandfather through Mother's second and third marriages; by the fourth marriage we were in college. Grandfather died shortly before I graduated, and I got a place of my own not long after that.

I've never thought of the house as belonging to me in any way. It isn't really the kind of house that *can* belong to anyone other than its creator; it was Great-Grandfather's house, and the rest of us just lived there for a while. Jase and I have privately agreed that when in due course we have to assume ownership, we'll let the house pass into historical preservation or else sell it and give the money to some reputable charity listed in the yellow pages.

I have, as I've said, stocks and bonds due to Grandfather, but I'm not real comfortable with the income. I can't see that I did anything to earn the money, and I don't much like the idea of enjoying a free ride at the expense of an ancestor—especially when he didn't get to enjoy the money when he was alive.

So, despite growing up in a mini-castle with somewhat opulent and peculiar furnishings, I have never belonged to what you'd call the rich set. And even when Mother could have afforded it, she had flatly refused to allow either Jase or me to do "society things" like join country clubs, own sleek little sports cars, or throw unsupervised parties. Just to emphasize the point, she had also shipped us off to Uncle Cain's ranch in Wyoming every summer, where we worked very hard.

My mother is a very complicated woman. She didn't allow me to do society things, yet she made me "come out" into society as soon as I turned eighteen (an incident I have almost convinced myself never happened). She made damned sure I understood that money was something one earned—even though, quite bluntly, she married it. If you understand her, how about giving me a clue.

I WAS SORT of hoping Trey and I would reach the refuge of our room without encountering any of the family (I wanted to recruit my energy). But we'd covered no more than the ground floor when my mother came down the stairs and met us in the entrance hall.

Mother is a lovely woman—and she doesn't look her age. Her black hair is as thick and shiny as it was in her youth, and elegantly styled in a medium length not many women past fifty could get away with. That day, her makeup was understated, and her dress flattered a figure that hadn't changed by more than an inch or two in thirty-five years.

We are the same height, five four, which places us in the small-to-average group for women. Her green eyes are both brighter and lighter in shade than mine, I think, and her features are a bit more delicate. And, though I never hear it myself, Jason says that Mother and I sound very much alike, except that her southern accent is much stronger than mine (despite the fact that she'd trotted around the globe for nearly twenty years, while I'd spent the vast majority of my life in Atlanta).

"Lane, you look wonderful," she said, smiling, as she came down the stairs toward us.

I didn't run up to meet her—and for the same reason she'd started talking before she reached me. We were somewhat stiff with each other, Mother and I. We'd been that way since I was a child, and twenty years later our undemonstrative greetings had become more than a little ingrained. I have to admit, though, that I hadn't exactly tried to close the distance between us.

We didn't really hug, even though it had been months since we'd last been together; she sort of touched my shoulders and brushed her cheek against mine. We were both smiling. We were always very polite, Mother and I.

"Thanks. You look great as usual," I said. "Mother, this is Trey Fortier. Trey, my mother, Elizabeth Rowland." I didn't stumble over her new married name, even though it was the first time I'd said it aloud. Practice, which I'd had a lot of, tends to eliminate those little awkward hesitations.

"Trey, I've heard a lot about you," my mother said pleasantly, offering her hand. I wondered at her nerve; I sure as hell hadn't told her anything about him. "I hope you'll make yourself at home this weekend."

"Thank you, I'm happy to be here," Trey replied in his most charming voice (definitely not his cop voice) as they shook hands. "And my best wishes on your marriage."

I realized only then, when she glanced at me, that I hadn't wished Mother well. I should have, of course, but my good wishes hadn't helped any of her previous marriages.

She inclined her head slightly to accept Trey's best wishes. "Adam wanted to be here to meet you both, but he had to take a call from his partner in London. Business won't wait, I'm afraid."

"What does he do?" Trey asked.

"He's a lawyer—or barrister as they say over there. He hopes his son will take over for him in a few years, but David has only recently joined the firm, so I imagine we'll be shuttling there and back for a while yet."

Mother hadn't been forthcoming about the children of her new spouse; that was the first I'd heard of David Rowland. Not that I especially wanted to meet him; I have stepsiblings all over the world, several of whom I don't know.

"David had to remain in London," Mother added, then looked at me. "But Vanessa was able to be here. I hope you'll like her, Lane."

Just from the phrasing, I doubted it. And there was an almost imperceptible note in Mother's voice I'd learned to recognize; she liked David, but wasn't at all fond of Vanessa.

"I'm sure we'll get along," I said politely. I was always polite with Mother, remember?

She smiled quickly. "I'm sure you will. Did Alexander have your bags taken up?"

"Of course. I've shown Trey the first floor; we were just on our way up. Drinks in the living room at seven, as usual?"

Mother nodded, graciously accepting my rather blunt dismissal. "I'll see you two then," she said, and headed across the entrance hall. Toward the kitchen, I guessed.

As we began climbing the stairs to the second floor, Trey said, "You and your mother aren't exactly close, are you?"

"Oh, you noticed that?"

"Don't be a smartass, Montana."

I shrugged. "No, we aren't especially close. It isn't a tragedy."

He glanced at me when we reached the landing. "So how do you feel about a stepfather?"

"Since Adam Rowland is stepfather number seven," I said dryly, "I don't feel much of anything. I've learned not to. That way, the divorce won't be painful."

"Your mother has been married eight times?" It obviously startled him.

"Yep. And never widowed." I could have bitten my tongue when he glanced at me again and I realized he was wondering about my father. Perfectly natural, but you may have noticed I didn't want to talk about my father. In fact, I felt a ridiculously panicked urge to change the subject as fast as possible.

Luckily for me, we reached our suite just then, and other things occupied Trey's attention.

I watched his face as he took a long look around. The sitting room was furnished with good, heavy furniture, and owed its brightness to pale materials for cushions, drapes, and rugs scattered across the polished hardwood floor. And the Palladian window, ten feet tall, helped. (There wasn't a ceiling in the house under fifteen feet.)

The bathroom was immense, and the plumbing, up-

dated ten years ago, featured a sunken tub large enough
for a party of four, as well as a steam shower.

But the bedroom . . . Ah, the bedroom. This had
been my favorite bedroom—even though I'd never slept
in it. It was so ridiculous it was fascinating. Ankle-deep
carpeting stretched wall to wall, as white as snow. The
wallpaper was a rich scarlet with gold embossing. The
big windows (not Palladian) were curtained in sheer,
gauzy whiteness; there was one on each side of the bed,
and both had window seats with scarlet cushions. Two
gigantic wardrobes stood against the walls on either
side of the bathroom door, their bleached-oak wood-
work intricately carved, principally with rosebuds and
cherubs. A dressing mirror, also of bleached oak, stood
in one corner: two fat cherubs held the mirror.

There was also a sultan's-favorite-girl chaise complete with carved cherubs and hearts, and boasting
scarlet cushions; and a scarlet velvet wing-backed chair
obviously for the male guest (scarlet footstool thoughtfully provided). Those two articles flanked the pale
marble fireplace. The nightstands on either side of the
bed were also bleached oak, carved intricately (you can
guess with what). Which brings me to . . .

The bed. That should be spelled in caps, actually.
THE BED.

Trey walked slowly to this structure, his face so un-
consciously fascinated I nearly giggled. When he stood
beside it, the mattress came up to his waist, which
meant I would have to make use of the little scarlet
stool and climb to get into the thing.

King-size beds of today would hang their heads in
shame. Not only was this specimen a four-poster with
a gauzy white canopy, and not only would it sleep six
or seven people without undue crowding, but it was

graced by cherubs holding the draped gauze of the canopy on all four of the intricately carved posts, the headboard (bleached oak, of course) was heart-shaped, and the elaborate canopy was supported high above by a large cupid—apparently flying without visible means of support and clutching white gauze in his fat little fingers.

Trey looked at the cherub on the post nearest him, reached out one finger to touch a rounded wooden belly, and burst out laughing.

I'd heard him laugh like that only a couple of times; it was a nice sound. Enjoying it, I crossed the room to one of the wardrobes and opened it. I found my things neatly unpacked and knew Trey's belongings would be similarly disposed in the other wardrobe, then I closed the door and went to the bed.

"I would have warned you," I said. "But—how? Who could possibly be prepared for this room?"

"Nobody," Trey agreed, still chuckling. "My God, Montana, you had some peculiar relatives."

"Better make that present tense. Some of Mother's relatives have their moments."

He must have decided to form his own opinion about that, because he only shook his head slightly and said, "Are all the other bedrooms furnished like this one?"

"All of them are different. But I'd have to say they're just as peculiar. For instance, there's an Oriental suite, and an Italian one—Renaissance—and one done up like Spain at the height of the Inquisition, and . . . Well, you get the point."

Musingly, Trey said, "I'd love to see the Spanish Inquisition one."

"It's on the third floor. Jason's, probably; he usually

asks to have it. He says that room has a beneficial effect on his creativity.''

Trey eyed me. "You're serious?"

"Absolutely."

"I'll say it again, Montana. You had—and have—some peculiar relatives."

I didn't bother to defend Jason; he can take care of himself. "You won't get an argument," I said, and looked at my watch. "Well, we've got a couple of hours before we're expected downstairs for drinks. Since it's raining now, it's not the best time to show you around outside. So—"

Trey pulled me close and kissed me. I should like to state here that I had been at some pains to treat this affair of ours in a light (albeit careful) vein. Which means that I was casual whenever possible and tried not to make it obvious that certain actions of his reduced me to a state of mindless idiocy. Sometimes I even tried to carry on a conversation when blissful silence would have been my preference.

"It's this bed, isn't it? You've spotted all the erotic carvings among the hearts and cherubs, and it's turning you on."

"A cop's eye for detail."

"Just don't get too many ideas. Some of those carvings represent illegal acts, and we mustn't forget you're an officer of the law—"

"Shut up, Montana."

TWO

IT WASN'T exactly accidental that Trey and I went downstairs a little early; I planned it that way. As far as I'm concerned, it's much less taxing to meet a bunch of people one or two at a time rather than walking into a roomful of them. Not that Trey was the least bit shy or unsure of himself—quite the contrary. I was the one who needed a little breathing space between relatives.

Jason was the lone occupant of the huge living room when we went in. He'd already fixed himself a drink from the bar set up near a front window, and was leaning against the back of a chair nearby.

"Hi, ya'll," he drawled.

"He gets very southern in this house," I told Trey.

"And she gets a little sarcastic," Jase retorted.

"I've noticed," Trey said.

Jason looked interested. "Which?"

"The sarcasm. But you are drawling, Jason." Trey and my brother have been comfortable with each other from the first time they met.

"It's Mother more than the house," Jason explained apologetically. "She sounds so damned southern you

17

expect a hoopskirt. Without meaning to, I get it in my ear, and before I know it I sound like a gent.''

"I do not get sarcastic just because I'm here," I announced, having thought about it. (Isn't self-delusion wonderful?) The men looked at me with identical expressions of polite contradiction; they had instantly (and apparently by telepathic agreement) formed a purely male solidarity. Like any woman would, I found it maddening.

"Stop looking at me like that. I don't.''

In a dry tone, Jase said, "Lanie, if I painted you right now, you'd be an abstract. And the colors would be chaotic.''

That comment isn't so obscure if you know that my brother is an artist. And since the credit is none of mine, I'll state here that he is immensely talented and will be famous someday. Jason has confidence without undue ego; he says he only hopes he's still alive to enjoy the tacky benefits of commercial success.

We have the same coloring: easily tanned skin, black hair, greenish eyes. We look very much brother and sister to the point of sometimes being mistaken for twins (bone structure, according to Jason), even though he's nine inches taller than me and gangly. I'm two years older than him, but Jase was born mature (in some ways, at least), and I've never really thought of him as my little brother.

By the way—only Jason calls me Lanie. I won't stand for it from anybody else.

"Well, you're not going to paint me and we both know it," I muttered, growing more and more uncomfortable to have the two men closest to me pondering my hang-ups.

"Why not?" Trey asked mildly.

I gave Jason a glare that promised great things along the lines of revenge if he dared answer that. The truth was that Jason had told me long ago he'd paint me only when I fell in love. He hadn't painted me yet. You may understand why I wasn't anxious to share that bit of information with Trey.

My brother and I are very close (unlike some siblings, we genuinely like each other), so Jase probably wouldn't have crossed the line even without my warning glare. Anyway, his answer was as mild as Trey's question.

"I'm not ready to paint her yet. Haven't painted Mother, either. Too close to the subjects, I suppose."

"Speaking of which—have you seen Mother?" I asked.

"Yeah, when I got here. Met Adam, too." In response to my raised eyebrow, Jason shrugged. "He's got my vote, Lanie. It's early, of course, but I like him."

Jason, more easygoing than me, had been fairly neutral about all our stepfathers, and tolerant of stepsiblings. But, then, other than a slight shyness around admiring women, Jase isn't the least bit insecure. I've always believed he fights his demons on canvas and in private, so those around him see only the peace after the storm.

"Then maybe she's struck gold this time," I said lightly.

Trey gave me a thoughtful look (probably heard the sarcasm), but before he could comment, two more people entered the room.

"Lane!" My uncle, Cain Buford, lifted me off my feet in a bear hug. I'm not demonstrative with many people, and I'd seen Cain only a couple of months before, but he'd always been sort of like a Saint Bernard puppy in his affection; when he grinned at you, you couldn't help but grin back.

He didn't look much like a rancher, but he did look a lot like Mother. He was a little above medium height, with thinning dark hair and smiling greenish eyes. But he was obviously strong, and he moved with the kind of ease you only see in people who lead very active lives. He had a peculiar drawl, partly southern and partly western, and such a friendly smile that a stranger would think he didn't have a temper. They'd be wrong, though. Cain didn't get mad often, but when he did it was a scary thing to watch.

By the time he put me back on my feet, my Aunt Maddy had hugged Jason and introduced herself to Trey. Before I could worry about introducing Trey to my uncle, they were taking care of that while Maddy came to me.

"Lane, is everything okay?" she asked softly.

I hugged her back and nodded reassuringly. The last time she'd seen me, a couple of months before, I hadn't been in what you'd call tiptop emotional shape. "Everything's fine."

She glanced aside at Trey, who was talking to Cain. "So he's the one. Now that I've met him, I can understand why you bolted out to the ranch a few months ago. Anybody can see he's a man a woman would have to take very seriously."

"Did Jason tell?" I demanded, albeit in a low voice.

Maddy was wearing her serene smile, but her blue eyes were glimmering with amusement. "He didn't have to. For God's sake, Lane, do you think Cain and I don't know you after all these years? We knew about the Townsend mess from the papers, and you told us you were involved in that, but we knew there was a man in there somewhere, and that he was the real reason you had to get away from Atlanta. Since you obviously didn't want to talk about it, we left you alone.''

Being Maddy, she didn't ask outright, which allowed me to treat the whole thing lightly.

''I just needed to think a few things through,'' I told her with a shrug. ''The Townsend investigation got kind of crazy there at the end, and I was too close. With Trey and me, the timing was lousy. I needed room to breathe.''

She smiled wryly. ''That's what Cain said when you turned up at the ranch. So we gave you the room. We've been wildly curious, though. When Elizabeth called about this get-together, she said it looked like you might be serious about someone. Knowing how cautious you are about men, we felt it had to be the same one.''

I definitely wasn't happy about Mother's perception (or crystal ball), but I didn't offer a sarcastic remark despite feeling threatened. That was a very difficult thing to do with Maddy. Be sarcastic, I mean. Slim, tanned, and elegant, she presented a picture of grace and peace which rarely failed to calm me, whatever my mood. People were nice to Maddy; she had that effect, even on strangers.

Cain and Maddy had done more than their share to raise Jase and me, since we'd spent every summer on their ranch from the time I was ten years old. Cain had set a good example of responsibility and hard work, and Maddy's serene gentleness was a motherly trait our own mother didn't have. They also gave me a dandy example (my only one, really) of what a good and stable marital relationship could be; they were very, very close, and very loving with each other.

"Lane, where's Choo?" Cain asked, moving behind the bar; he was the unofficial bartender of the family.

"Unless the cook's thrown him out by now, he's in the kitchen getting fat." I was glad of the change of subject.

"Cain brought him a catnip mouse," Maddy said, accepting a glass from her husband (as well as a kiss), and then sitting down in a nearby chair.

"I like Choo," Cain said quite unnecessarily. "He has a personality. What can I get you?" he asked me.

"Something soft. A Coke or juice will be fine."

He fixed a glass of Pepsi for me and a brandy for Trey, all the while telling us (mostly Trey) about a few of Choo's adventures out in Wyoming. Like the time my dauntless cat very nearly wound up in a bear trap with a somewhat agitated bear. And the time he thought it would be a good idea to hitch a ride on a Black Angus bull. You can guess what happened. Poor Choo; he didn't even last eight seconds.

Cain liked animals a lot, especially Choo.

I admit I was listening only halfway, but I still didn't hear Wanda come into the room. I didn't know she was there until she sidled up beside me in that disconcertingly furtive manner common to teens in a room full of adults and poked me with an elbow. She didn't *mean* to poke me, as was obvious from her words.

"I'm so clumsy! Sorry, Lane." She tried a tentative, hopeful smile.

I couldn't help but laugh. I hadn't seen my young cousin in several months, but it was obvious her situation hadn't improved in the meantime. Shortly before her fifteenth birthday, Wanda had shot up about six inches (making her two inches taller than me), and more than a year later, her body was still coping with the shock. She was all elbows and knees, with the awkwardness of any young creature maturing at an alarming rate.

"I know, sweetie, it's one of the many curses of being a teenager."

"Did you bump into things when you were my age?" she asked wistfully.

Jason snorted. "Lanie? She couldn't walk across a room without leaving chaos in her wake. Believe me, Wanda, you're a swan compared to our Lanie."

Family events are wonderful. Just wonderful.

"Quiet, Jase, or I'll tell a few stories on you," I warned, and cut off his inevitable response by performing my proper duty. "Wanda, this is Trey Fortier. Trey, my cousin, Wanda Hart."

She offered her hand with a stab at grown-up dignity, then immediately lapsed back into adolescence by blurting, "Lane's never brought a man here before."

Before I could blush (I almost never do, but he knows I can), Trey said, "Actually, I brought her. It's nice to meet you, Wanda."

Blushing furiously herself, Wanda muttered, "Likewise." She got her hand back from Trey, cleared her throat, and said brightly to me, "Have you met Vanessa yet?"

For a moment, I was at a loss, but then I remembered. My new stepsister. "No. What's she like?"

"Tall, blond, beautiful—and knows it. About the only thing she *does* know. Talk about an airhead!" Wanda pursed her lips, eyes dancing. "She's been giving poor Alexander a hard time since she got here. Her room's next to mine, so I've heard plenty. Her room is too cold, and there's a draft, and the bed's lumpy, and *why* does it take sooo long for someone to come when she rings—stuff like that. We should have Alexander canonized, Lane. Seriously.''

Before I could comment, a new voice spoke in a slightly chiding tone.

''Wanda, you can't possibly know someone you met an hour ago, at least not well enough to offer an opinion. Never make up your mind about someone the first time you meet them.''

''Oh, Mom,'' Wanda said, rolling her eyes as she accepted a Coke from Cain.

First impression or not, I placed a good deal of trust in Wanda's opinion of my new stepsister. Despite her tendency to blurt out whatever she was thinking, she had a peculiar talent for understanding people. But I didn't say anything about that aloud; instead, I introduced Trey to my mother's sister, Kerry Hart, and her husband, Baxter.

Kerry, the middle of the three sisters, was the most even in temperament, with dark hair, greenish eyes, and a humorous outlook. Wanda looked like her, except that Wanda's dark hair held a few threads of silver at one temple; Baxter was prematurely gray, and he'd passed those genes on to their daughter.

Baxter, whipcord-lean and sun-browned, with a crooked smile, looked more like a rancher than Cain did. An insurance company V.P., he was just this side of a health nut, with a habit of running every morning. He was as easygoing as Kerry. They made a nice couple.

Both were polite to Trey and greeted me warmly, but they didn't linger at the bar after getting their drinks. Not that it mattered, because the room was beginning to fill up with the rest of my relatives. Since everybody came to the bar to get their drinks, that provided the opportunity for me to introduce Trey, and kept the conversations mercifully brief.

"Lane, dear, you're looking tired," Emily said by way of greeting, her gentle voice as sweet as always.

"It's the light," I said, because it never did any good to take offense at anything she said. "Emily, Lawrence, this is Trey Fortier. Trey, Emily and Lawrence Stoddard."

"Elizabeth's cousins on her mother's side," Emily explained, offering a small, plump hand. She looked older than her age (thirty-eight), her improbably red hair cut short around a pale, lined face. Her faded blue eyes were restless, flitting from face to face or object to object as if nothing could hold her attention for more than a few seconds.

Mother had once said that the tragedy of Emily's life was her inability to have children. Apparently, she'd desperately wanted to give Lawrence a son, and had suffered through all those horrendous tests and treatments inflicted on infertile women before it was finally determined that she would never be able to carry or give birth to a child. I'd never heard Emily mention the subject, but since her complaints tended to focus on trivial subjects, that wasn't surprising.

Some people can't face their true pain, so they pick away at little hurts and irritants. At least, so it seems to me.

Anyway.

"Cain, dear, fix me one of your special drinks? And my Larry will have scotch, as usual."

Her Larry was shaking hands with Trey and murmuring some mild greeting. His voice was rather deep, but toneless. He wasn't a bad-looking man; he had a healthy thatch of medium-brown hair, regular features, and a pleasant smile. But he wasn't exactly memorable either.

"How have you been, Lawrence?" I asked.

He seemed a little surprised to be addressed. "Fine, Lane, just fine. Busy."

"Are you still traveling all over the Southeast, or have they chained you to a desk?"

"Oh, I still have my route."

I tried again. "The market for computer software must be fairly brisk these days."

He nodded and smiled.

Emily handed him his glass just then and returned her attention to me, which meant I could give up on Lawrence. I was grateful. I didn't much like Emily, but at least she could keep a conversation going. (All by herself, actually.)

"Lane, dear, I probably shouldn't mention it, but that shade of purple really isn't your color."

I smiled with all my teeth. "Didn't you know, Emily? Purple is a universal color. Anybody can wear it. Like peach and turquoise."

She blinked at me. "Really? But it makes your eyes look so dark, dear."

I wanted to tell her that if my eyes were dark it was probably because the pupils had dilated. That happens when you're drugged or stressed out. Since I seldom even touch alcohol, you can guess which was my problem.

However, before I could get even more sarcastic, Trey intervened.

"That's a lovely necklace, Mrs. Stoddard."

Since one hand was tucked into Lawrence's arm and the other held her drink, Emily could only touch her diamond pendant with one beringed pinky. "Why, thank you! And call me Emily, dear. My Larry bought this for me on our anniversary. The chain is a bit short, but I love it.''

That comment was so perfectly Emily that I could only admire it in silence. She loved the gift, but couldn't resist a sweetly uttered criticism.

Emily finally decided that she and her Larry should find a seat across the room, so they went. Lawrence hadn't said a word after my conversational gambits had failed, which wasn't unusual. He never said much.

When they'd gone, Trey stepped closer to me and murmured, ''I think you look great in purple.''

I took a sip of my Pepsi, sighed, and said, ''You're such a nice man.''

Since Cain was talking to Jason and Maddy, we were relatively alone for the moment. Trey kept his voice low anyway.

''And you're very tense. What's wrong, Montana? So far, your relatives seem like normal people to me. Is it the new stepfather you're anxious about?''

I didn't much like that adjective. I wasn't *anxious*. Tense, yes. ''I told you, I don't feel much of anything about new stepfathers,'' I reminded him. ''If I'm uptight, it's because the worst is yet to come. My least favorite relative should be making his appearance any time now.''

''And that person is—?''

''A pain in the ass.''

Trey lifted an eyebrow at me, but we were interrupted before he could comment.

''Cain, can I have a rum and Coke? Oh—hi, Lane.''

''Hi, Peter.'' I introduced another of my cousins to Trey, not surprised to see that Peter was in a rotten mood.

He had inherited his father's curiously disconcerting sensual features, but on Peter they were almost delicate; he was, truly, a beautiful young man. Think of Byron: lots of dark, loosely curling hair; huge, expressive dark eyes; and the tormented look of soulful suffering. (I'm not mocking him; he really *did* look like he'd endured a great deal in his short life.) He had a cupid mouth held almost perpetually in a sulky curve, bit his nails to the quick (I could sympathize; it was a habit I was struggling to break), and was one of the most physically nervous people I'd ever known.

He made reasonably polite noises during the introduction and offered his hand, looking at Trey with faint interest that surprised me; Peter was generally disinterested in anything other than his own troubles, and since he was still scowling faintly I knew he was upset.

"When did you get in?" I asked. (Yes, I know, but when you don't care much for your relatives, polite platitudes are about all you can summon.)

"A few hours ago," he replied, one hand resting on the bar and long fingers beating out a jittery tattoo against the polished wood. "Lane, did you bring your car?"

"No, Trey drove."

Mildly, Trey said, "You're welcome to borrow it, Peter."

If I could have done it unobtrusively, I would have nudged or pinched Trey; Peter was a competent driver when he wasn't upset, but he usually was. Upset, I mean. My battered station wagon was one thing; Trey's Mercedes was something else. But when Peter's beautiful, sullen face brightened, I didn't have the heart to come up with some excuse.

Besides, Trey was insured.

"Thanks," Peter said gratefully. "I don't need it right now, but I thought I might drive into the city tomorrow morning. Dad's so fussy about his car, I hate to even ask him."

"Any time," Trey told my cousin. He was too well-mannered to wonder aloud why this twenty-five-year-old man hadn't driven his own car here but had ridden with his parents.

Come to think of it, I wasn't even sure Peter *had* a car of his own.

Jason came back to the bar to get his drink freshened just then, and Peter turned away stiffly without another word. My brother gave me a wry look, which I returned. Peter was reasonably neutral about me, but he actively disliked Jason and didn't bother hiding it. Jase hadn't said much about it to me, but I'd always thought the reason was pure jealousy. Peter was firmly under his father's thumb, no money of his own, no career or woman in his life (despite his good looks) and, as far as we knew, no talent to call his own, and his sulks tended to make the people around him uncomfortable. Jason was independent, talented, well-liked, very much his own man, and extremely popular with women.

"Private feud?" Trey asked quietly.

Jason shrugged. "We can't pick our relatives, unfortunately, and they can't pick us. To tell you the truth, I feel sorry for the poor bastard. If I had to live with Innis, I'd probably have a grudge against the world, too." He glanced at me. "Have you told Trey—?"

"About Innis?" I shook my head. "He'll find out the awful truth soon enough, I'm afraid."

Trey was smiling slightly. "He can't be that bad."

"Just wait," Jason advised. "If he doesn't offend you with the first word out of his mouth, the second one will do it. My only consolation is that he's not a blood relative; I'd hate to think we belonged to the same gene pool.''

Having stated his opinion, Jason went back toward Maddy with his refilled glass. Personally, I think he'd seen Innis in the doorway and was escaping, but to this day Jase denies that.

When they crossed the room to the bar, Innis was, as usual, walking a pace ahead of his wife. Ignoring that, I quite deliberately gave my aunt precedence.

''Grace, I'd like you to meet Trey Fortier. Trey, my Aunt Grace, Mother's youngest sister. And this is her husband, Innis Langdon.''

It was the best slap in the face I could manage without being openly rude; I'd had manners drummed into me at an early age, and really found it difficult to be as discourteous as I wanted to be. Innis deserved the worst.

Grace offered a tentative hand to Trey while Innis glared at me. I didn't avoid that hostile stare, though I'll admit it wasn't easy. I would have preferred to look away.

Innis was a strange man in many ways. In height and build he was average, though in excellent physical shape. His hair was dark and thick. Women seemed to find him attractive, or compelling in a sexual way, judging by what I'd seen and heard over the years. Maybe I was a rare exception, or maybe I just knew him too well to find anything about him attractive.

Anyway. His handsome face was heavy-featured and almost shockingly sensual; the effect was rather like looking at a painting in which the sins of avarice and lechery had been etched in a face that had meant to be more than usually attractive. It was unnerving, and made me a little queasy, which was why I found it difficult to look at him.

Grace, on the other hand, was almost like a negative. She had the family coloring, but time—or Innis—hadn't been kind. Her dark hair was graying, and the beauty that had once outshone her sisters' in their youth had been squeezed from her pinched features years before. Even her big green eyes had faded to a sort of olive drab.

Have you ever met a real, honest-to-God martyr? After watching her for years, I'd come to the conclusion that my Aunt Grace was just that. The only reason I could figure why she stayed with Innis was because she was earning points to get into heaven.

"It's a pleasure to meet you," she told Trey, sounding, as usual, breathless and unsure of herself. Like Lawrence, she didn't talk very much; unlike him, she never seemed comfortable or untroubled by her surroundings.

Innis, never one to be ignored for long, chose to needle me rather than greet Trey. "You mean he came with you? You actually brought a man home to meet the family?"

Cain broke in before I could frame a suitable response. "Scotch, as usual, Innis?"

"Yeah, and make it a double."

Grace never drank, and when Innis took his glass from Cain and went across the room toward their son, she followed as if the leash were visible.

Almost immediately, Innis said something to Peter that brought a hot flush to my cousin's face. They were too far away for those of us by the bar to hear, but it was obvious they were beginning one of their frequent arguments.

In the all-too-brief interval before it became impossible to ignore them, I said to Trey, "Family events are wonderful, don't you think?"

". . . how can I grow up when you won't let me?" Peter shouted suddenly, his features reddened and twisted in rage.

I didn't have to know how the argument had started to know the gist of it. Peter had probably asked his father for money to invest in some new business venture, and Innis had promptly refused—undoubtedly using words calculated to tear his son's fragile ego to shreds. It might have happened a week ago; now that Innis had an audience, and since he enjoyed nothing better than loudly destroying someone—particularly his son—he had probably brought up the subject himself. And Peter, true to character, took the bait hook, line, and sinker.

Innis's voice boomed easily across the room—not an undignified shout like Peter's—cutting with contempt. "You're a fool. What the hell do you know about the video marketing business? Do you think you can shoot a few home movies and get rich?"

"If you'd just *listen*—"

"I have better things to do than listen to your pathetic attempts to cultivate a business mind," Innis snapped.

"John says—"

"John Howard? That idiot? Christ, Peter, he's more stupid than you are—if that's possible."

I couldn't help but wince. Peter wasn't a particularly lovable young man, but I had a certain amount of sympathy for him; I'd decided years ago that it really must have been hell living under Innis's thumb. Still, if Peter only had the sense—and guts—to strike out on his own . . .

As usual, most of the family members were looking elsewhere and affecting deafness. Trey, however, was watching the two rather narrowly. It must have been the cop in him, alert to trouble and ready to step in if need be. But Peter was running true to form that day; white with rage, he tried to speak, failed, then turned and stormed out of the room.

He usually did that, more out of a helpless fury, I thought, than anything else. And the fact that it was a weak ending to an argument made it even worse for Peter. The confrontations with Innis—the public ones, I mean—had been going on for nearly ten years, and Peter never seemed embarrassed by them. In fact, he often tried, at some point, to enlist the support of the remainder of the family against his father. Speaking for myself, I was always tempted, but tried to stay out of it. Judging by the response of the others, I had decided they felt the same way.

So, the most recent bout ended in Innis's triumph as Peter escaped. Alexander would probably find him and coax him into the dining room when dinner was announced, I thought. He usually did. As for Innis, he stood there smirking and looking around the room as if he expected applause.

"Act two," I murmured into the brief silence, just as Grace rose from her chair with a distressed look on her face, and Emily drew an audible breath to begin one of her monologues.

As usual after one of Innis and Peter's fights, Grace was drifting around the room smiling hesitantly and apologetically, as if by looking each of us in the eye at least once she could somehow allay the discomfort of strife. It only served to keep the tension high, I thought, because her martyred expression was more than a little maddening.

I have a hard time understanding people who suffer bravely in silence. Me, I'd kick and scream. And my first target would be Innis's most tender and valued spot.

Anyway, while Grace prowled the room, Emily was holding forth in her gentle, complaining voice (it had a peculiar carrying quality), her small hands fluttering aimlessly.

"I just don't understand why dear Elizabeth spends so much time traveling when she could be here. Such a marvelous old house. She should really stay home to supervise the servants. Why, the rugs in our room are actually *frayed,* and the silk on one chair is beginning to split. I really don't understand . . ."

In case you haven't noticed, Emily called everybody *dear.* Except for her husband. Lawrence was always her Larry. He got the possessive while the rest of us got the affectionate.

I looked at Lawrence beside Emily on the couch, and remembered my attempt to get a decent conversation going. It had been like talking to someone who was listening to a ballgame on his Walkman, or who was slightly deaf and pretending not to be.

I didn't feel much about him either way, good or bad. But I think I did have a vague sort of contempt for him, which upset me far more than it (probably) would have him. I can't really explain it except to say that he seemed to me a complete nonentity; I always felt a faint surprise to notice he was in the room.

Yes, I know. That's not very nice. But I'm trying to be honest here. And, as far as I can remember, nobody else noticed Lawrence very much—except as a silent extension of Emily. He was neat and quiet and considerate as a guest, never causing the household staff trouble or setting any of the family members at odds with one another. He said please and thank you. He invariably put a coaster under his glass, folded his napkin after eating, and wiped his shoes on the mat—whether it was wet out or not.

But he never made much of an impression, either positive or negative. He just sort of . . . took up space.

Even though it galls me to admit it, as much as I disliked Innis, at least he made people think—and feel—about him. You always knew Innis was in the room. Always.

Lawrence sat there beside Emily, smiling and silent, with his scotch glass neatly on a coaster, every medium-brown hair on his head in place. He seemed so blandly content that I couldn't help wondering if he'd gone on some kind of medication in the early days of his marriage. (Yes, that's even less nice, I know.) Anyway, he seemed completely untroubled by the preceding scene between Innis and Peter, and by the way his wife went on complaining gently to the room at large.

In a low voice to me, Wanda suddenly said, ''Peter's really upset this time.''

I tuned out Emily, which wasn't very difficult (maybe that was Lawrence's secret?), and turned my attention to my cousin, who had snuck up on me again. She looked anxious. ''What, about this video business?'' I asked.

Wanda hesitated, biting her lip, then said, ''I was upstairs about an hour ago, and when I looked out my window I saw Peter arguing with Innis down by the cars. Maybe it was the beginning of this fight, I don't know, but . . . Lane, Peter tried to hit Innis.''

I didn't have to ask if he'd succeeded; Peter was as

ineffectual physically as he was verbally. Nevertheless, the fact that he'd tried—a first as far as I knew—didn't bode at all well for the next two days.

As I've said, family gatherings are wonderful.

Trying to reassure my cousin, I said, "They've been fighting nearly as long as you've been alive, Wanda, and nothing drastic's happened so far. With a little luck . . ."

Cain gave a wry chuckle as he joined the conversation. "With a little luck we'll get through the weekend without a free-for-all. Is that what you mean, Lane?"

"Close enough," I said.

Wanda didn't appear noticeably reassured. "Well, all I know is that when Peter came back into the house he looked like he could have killed somebody. I sure didn't want to get in his way." She shrugged.

I would have tried another stab at reassurance (not that I felt much myself), but the remainder of our little house party came into the room just then and quite effectively distracted me.

As an entrance, it was typical of Mother. She came in on the arm of her new husband, her face glowing. She looked extremely happy, and since this marriage was more than a couple of months old, that was a positive sign.

I looked with interest at my new stepfather. I pegged Adam Rowland in his mid-fifties. He had thick blond hair going silver at the temples, an outdoor tan (as opposed to one earned beneath sunlamps), and very steady, faintly amused blue eyes. He looked to be in excellent shape physically. He was also tall—about the same height as both Trey and Jason, which made the three of them the tallest men in the room by several inches.

Innis would hate that, I thought with an inner laugh. He was five ten, and he could never hide his dislike of having to look up to meet another man's eyes.

Pushing that out of my mind, I looked beyond Mother and Adam to see my new stepsister, who was just behind them. Wanda had been right. Vanessa was tall, leggy, and blond. About twenty-five or so, and model-gorgeous. Damn it, she looked just like those advertiser-examples of youth and beauty to which we're all subjected with every magazine, commercial, and billboard.

Except that her nose was—just faintly—crooked.

Yeah, I know. Meow. Really, though, I usually don't get hostile when I'm confronted by a woman who's everything I'm not. Really. But that crooked nose of hers was elevated in a way that I—or any other woman—could instantly recognize as a sign of haughty superiority, and I tend to bristle when anybody waves that attitude at me.

Thinking you're better than everyone else isn't only asinine, it's incredibly boring.

Anyway. Mother took one quick glance around the room, then headed straight for me. That made sense. Since Jase had already met Adam, it was clearly my turn. Okay, fine.

"Lane, this is Adam," she said simply.

"Hello, Adam," I responded in my most polite tone. He didn't offer to kiss me, for which I was grateful, but simply shook hands. His hand was warm, his handshake firm, and his level gaze friendly.

"It's nice to meet you, Lane. I've heard a lot about you." His voice was rock-steady and peculiarly calming (maybe it was the English accent).

I felt a bit reassured. Already he was a vast improvement on the previous stepfather, who had not been pleased to find himself with two grown stepchildren. ''I'm looking forward to getting to know you.''

I'm ashamed to admit it, but that last was sort of a double-edged comment. With some of Mother's past marriages, I'd barely learned a new stepfather's name, much less anything else about him. It was just the kind of comment which, in the past, had caused Mother to bristle. This time, she merely smiled.

I managed to respond politely to the introduction to Vanessa, who looked down her crooked nose at me and said hello in a bored tone; and to introduce Trey, who was, as usual, calm and courteous. Somewhere in there, among the hellos and handshakes, Jason was introduced to Vanessa, who brightened noticeably.

Somehow or other, the group near the bar rearranged itself in the next few moments, rather to my alarm. Wanda joined her parents across the room. Cain was busy fixing drinks, so he was occupied. Vanessa was talking to Jason, with Maddy an interested listener, Adam was talking to Trey, and Mother and I were left confronting each other. I took refuge in my Pepsi.

However, no one has ever called my mother faint-hearted.

''Lane, you should have called me when you were involved in Jeffrey Townsend's murder a few months ago,'' she said.

''I wasn't involved in his murder,'' I answered automatically. ''Only the investigation. And it was all over in a week.''

''Not all of it,'' she noted with a slight nod toward Trey.

''How did you find out about him?'' I demanded— probably a bit fiercely.

Calmly, Mother replied, "I still have friends in Atlanta. One of them saw you and Trey out together a few times, and wrote to me about six weeks ago."

"And I suppose it was easy to find out who he was and where he worked. What'd she do, copy down his license plate number?" I muttered.

Mother smiled faintly. "No, she happened to recognize him from a news broadcast."

That figured. Murder was depressingly frequent news in Atlanta, and aside from being a regular spokesperson for his department, Trey was a favorite of the TV newspeople; the camera loved him, and he was always a polite interview—whether he answered their questions or not.

"Well, just do me a favor and don't assume anything, all right?" I said to my mother. "We're here because you went around me to invite Trey. My relationship with him is my business."

"I know that, Lane."

"Good. Then we understand each other." We were both smiling. But I'd drawn a line in the sand between us, and dared her to cross it.

THREE

DINNER was relatively pleasant, except for Innis's constant attempts to dominate the conversation—with individuals as well as the entire group. Alexander had, as I'd expected, persuaded Peter to join us at the table, and except for furious glances at his father, he kept mostly silent.

I didn't say much myself. I did notice a few other things, though. Adam was quiet, pleasant, and obviously intelligent. He was very attentive to Mother, yet also managed to speak to everyone else—and he was polite to Innis despite my dear uncle's belligerent attempts to get some kind of fight going.

Vanessa made two attempts—right under my nose, so to speak—to flirt with Trey, encountered bland courtesy from him (and at least one warning smile from me, as I recall), and turned her attention to Jason.

Innis began to loudly criticize insurance companies to Baxter (who was a V.P. at an insurance company), calling the business and those who perpetuated it criminals.

Baxter, smiling, advised him to write to his representatives in Washington.

By the time dessert was served, Jason looked like a hunted man. (He obviously wanted to be nice to Vanessa for Mother's sake, but his eyes were glazing over.)

Wanda tried to talk to Peter, who was seated beside her, and got nothing for her trouble except sullen monosyllables.

Innis began to needle Cain, apparently unable to understand why anyone would want to be in the dirty, sweaty business of ranching (Innis was a stockbroker and, to hear him tell it, that was the only job in the world worth having).

Cain snapped back a reply once, but regained control when Maddy touched his hand gently.

All in all, it was a normal family dinner.

The afterward was normal as well. We returned to the living room, where almost all of us remained for about an hour. Peter slid out fairly early, looking as if he wanted to find something he could break with his bare hands. Wanda began playing with Choo, who had finally emerged from the kitchen (with such a satisfied expression on his furry face that I knew he'd eaten far more than was good for him and would probably get sick before the night was over). Emily eyed my cat uneasily while he kept glancing at her; I didn't think she had a phobia, but it was borderline, and Choo, in the way of cats, knew or felt her dislike.

A few words here, if I may, about my cat. Siamese cats are known for their decided personalities, and mine has a number of quirks and traits all his own. First, as with humankind, he tends to like people who like him. Second, he is a good barometer of the mood of any group in which he finds himself. Third, he is a scene-stealer of the first order, drawing attention easily and holding it—even if he isn't doing anything. And, fourth, he is an extremely polite cat, greeting everyone in a room whether or not he likes them.

All the above points were illustrated that evening. When Choo came into the room, he greeted Trey and me first (I was sitting in a chair, and Trey on the arm of it). His greeting at such times was always the same to each person, sort of a long, drawn-out "Yaaaahh" sound. I responded with a mild hello, and Trey, always comfortable with cats in general and mine in particular, did likewise.

Choo moved around the room clockwise, greeting each person. He was visibly jittery (barometer reading: it was not a happy or relaxed group), and didn't linger after addressing someone he disliked. Innis, for instance, who replied to the greeting by staring down at Choo and declaring that he hated cats. Emily, Peter, Vanessa, and Lawrence also received short greetings. Peter ignored him, Vanessa looked disdainful, Emily replied in the nervous voice common to those who dislike cats (she actually addressed my cat as "dear Choo," if you can believe it), and Lawrence seemed mildly surprised. Everyone else was greeted with affection, particularly Mother, who bent forward in her chair to scratch the always-itchy place behind Choo's left ear.

My cat then allowed Wanda to occupy his attention with the catnip mouse Cain had brought for him, while the humans in the room watched him and talked desultorily. Peter left about that time, though I thought Trey and I were the only ones who noticed. We were sitting over near the bar, in the chair Maddy had occupied earlier, somewhat apart from the others.

The interlude might have remained reasonably peaceful, except that Innis decided to belittle my brother because he was an artist. I didn't like that, and neither did Mother (I saw her stiffen), but at least both of us knew Jason could take care of himself. And he did.

After the attack, Jason waited with a faint smile until the silence grated on Innis's nerves (like all bullies, he was always after a response), and calmly recited a list of male artists who had changed the world and/or memorably portrayed the times in which they'd lived, beginning with Michelangelo and ending with Norman Rockwell.

Getting into the spirit of the thing, I threw in a couple of artists Jason had overlooked—and nearly everyone else followed suit. Trey, Adam, Mother, Cain, Maddy, Kerry, and Baxter all contributed the name of a famous artist. Then Wanda solemnly offered the name of her seventh-grade art teacher, and we all laughed.

Innis fumed.

It wasn't all that late, but the gathering broke up shortly afterward. I think every one of us wanted to get away; I know I did. Wanda asked my permission, then took Choo off to her room. I reminded her to make sure he could get out of her room if he needed to, and Trey and I went to our own rooms alone.

I didn't ask Trey about his opinion of the family, figuring he'd offer it if he wanted to. Somewhat to my surprise, all he said on the subject as we were getting ready for bed was a question about Peter.

"Is he always so angry?"

"More with every year that passes," I answered. "Why?"

Trey shook his head slightly. "I don't like the look of him, Montana. He's ready to snap."

"And do something we'd all be sorry for?" I paused with one foot on the little scarlet stool and thought about it. "I shouldn't think he'd have the guts." Climbing into the bed, I added dryly, "To be perfectly honest, though, no one in this house would be particularly surprised—or grieve very much—if we found dear old Innis with a knife in his back."

THE WEATHER BROKE during the night, thankfully. We were greeted on Saturday with clearing skies and comfortably cool temperatures, which meant we wouldn't be cooped up in the house. There was a tennis court in fair shape, half a dozen horses available for riding, and a pleasantly landscaped garden with paths for strolling behind the house.

In other words, there was enough to do so that we wouldn't get in each other's hair during the day.

Usually, I was likely to miss breakfast altogether, since I am definitely not a morning person. On that bright Saturday, however, I was awake early. Trey was responsible (he definitely *is* a morning person). Actually, his mustache was responsible. It tickled. I sleep like the dead, and I can easily resist being prodded, shaken, or yelled at—though I eventually respond when Choo walks on me. But if you tickle me (a fact Trey had recently discovered), I am going to wake up.

I might have been a bit disgruntled about it, because I really do hate being awakened before I'm ready, but Trey was so creative that I was enjoying myself before I remembered to be irritated.

It was rare that I woke up with Trey due to the post-midnight demands of various crimes to which he had to attend, so it was definitely nice to have him all to myself for a change. And since it was the rule of the house that nobody was to be disturbed in the morning unless they rang for something or left the hall door standing open (considered a tacit invitation), we weren't interrupted.

"It's the bed," I declared a considerable time later as I was sitting on the subject in question, putting on my Reeboks. "You woke up at dawn, as usual, and there was nothing else to do but study the erotic carvings."

Trey was shaving, and through the open bathroom door, he said, "It was not the bed. I wanted to talk to you, and so far I've found only one way of waking you up. It worked so well I lost interest in conversation."

I couldn't help but grin to myself. "Well, what did you want to talk about?"

He peered around the doorjamb, his face half-lathered, and lifted an eyebrow at me. "Your mother."

"What about her?"

Trey went on with his shaving as he looked across the room at me, which made me a little nervous. I'd seen Jason do the same thing, and I never could understand why they didn't worry about amputating an earlobe or something.

"Of all the people in this house, I get the feeling it's your approval she wants most," he said finally.

"Hey, shouldn't you keep both eyes on the road?"

"Montana, I've been shaving for twenty years; I think I know how to do it by now."

"Yeah, but blind? That's why they put mirrors above sinks in bathrooms, you know, so men can see themselves shaving and women get their lipstick on straight."

"Why are you avoiding the subject of your mother?"

My lousy poker face is enough of a trial; I also have a difficult time being subtle when I don't want to talk about something.

Dangling my jean-clad legs over the side of the bed (Reeboks some distance above the floor), I sighed. "Because I don't want to talk about her. Trey, my mother and I have been at odds for most of my life. We get on each other's nerves in the worst way. We're not comfortable with each other. Like I told you yesterday, it's not a tragedy."

"Then why are you so tense about it?" he asked mildly.

"Tense? Me? You're imagining things."

He didn't reply to that, just continued to watch me steadily. After a few moments, I started to get antsy.

"You're looking at me with your cop's eyes," I accused him. "Quit it."

Trey smiled slightly, but those luminous eyes of his remained a little harder than I liked. It was something we ran into during the Townsend investigation; as much as he was a man, Trey was also a cop—and cops always try to get at the truth. He'd disconcerted me more than once by turning into a cop while I'd been thinking of him as a man, and I didn't much like the sensation.

Slowly, he said, "I'm just wondering why you'd rather fight with your mother than make peace."

Talk about being disconcerted. "That's ridiculous," I said. "We aren't having a war." Before he could go on worrying the subject, I changed it. "Since you woke me up so early, I want breakfast. Are you nearly done in there?"

"Five minutes," he replied, and went back to his mirror.

I knew he hadn't abandoned the subject forever. It might have been a sign of our diffident relationship, but at least a few times in the previous weeks, one or both of us had cautiously backed away from something that had hit a nerve. For instance, we had never really dealt with what nearly ended our relationship when it had barely begun—during the Townsend case.

There's no clear way to explain it to you—especially since we hadn't explained it to *us*. If you know the Townsend story, maybe you understand; if not, all I can say is that Trey being a cop and me being a suspect had caused a whole lot of problems. In the beginning, he had used me the way any good cop uses what he has to solve a case, and the result had been painful for us both. Near the end, I had lashed out at him, and I'd hurt him, because I was hurting.

It wasn't something I was particularly proud of. I certainly hadn't been anxious to bring up the subject again, and I hoped the issue was more or less a dead one. I mean, it wasn't likely we'd both be involved in another murder investigation, so we didn't have to thrash out that particular dilemma.

The problem with hiding your head in the sand like an ostrich is that, sooner or later, you're going to get blindsided.

Anyway, because we were still being careful with each other, Trey obviously knew better than to pursue the subject of my relationship with Mother. I was glad; even the little that had been said had made me uncomfortable. I had long ago decided that emotional ties were hideously complicated and seldom rational—which pretty much describes my feelings about Mother.

So I didn't say anything else about that. Instead, as we were preparing to leave our rooms, I said, "I just noticed—you don't have your beeper."

"No," he agreed. "Rudy knows where I am if there's an emergency."

Rudy was Sergeant Rudy Flint, Trey's second-in-command at work. I liked Rudy, and I think he liked me—although we can never really be sure how others feel about us. He'd been a bit stiff with me once (when I hurt Trey), and I'd cussed at him a couple of times for badly timed phone calls when Trey hadn't been wearing his beeper, but we generally got along.

In a way, I sort of hoped there would be an emergency serious enough for Rudy to summon Trey back to work. Not that I wanted anybody to die, and I was glad we were able to spend a weekend together (we never had until then). It was just that I was feeling unsettled and oddly trapped at that moment.

Those emotional ties. They were all around me, and a lot of them were too tight. I mean, it's fairly easy to be careful in a relationship when there's no outside interference, but when there are a number of people around you it gets tougher. Right then, I could have done without my assorted relatives.

One of them was in the hall when we left our rooms, and it was pretty obvious that Peter had been lying in wait. It was also obvious that he was still upset.

Without so much as a good morning, he said, "Trey, if you really meant I could borrow your car—"

"Sure," Trey said, and stepped back into our room to get his keys.

Briefly alone with Peter, I studied his pale face and felt the first real pang of worry. He didn't look good, as if he hadn't slept at all. Sympathetically, I said, "Don't take it so much to heart, Peter. Innis tears at all of us."

"Is that supposed to make me feel better?" he demanded, flushing hotly.

"No, I guess not. It must be hell to live with him."

"Taking my part, Lane? You never have before."

I shook my head slightly. "That isn't true; I'm on your side, I just don't want to fight with Innis."

"I'm tired of fighting with him," Peter muttered. "It's about time he started taking me seriously, and I mean to see to it he does."

Trey returned to my side just then. He didn't offer a comment on Peter's statement, just held out the keys. "It's the silver Mercedes," he said.

Peter looked momentarily perturbed, probably because of the expensive car, but then took the keys and mumbled a thanks.

I watched him stalk off down the hallway, then looked up at Trey. "The problem is," I remarked, "there's no way I can see for his situation to improve unless and until he gets out from under Innis's thumb. And he just *won't*. In his place, I think I'd join the army or something."

As we started for the stairs, Trey said, "I gather he doesn't have a job?"

"He's had a series of jobs. According to Peter—and judging by what I've seen myself—Innis always ruins it in one way or another. Either he makes sure Peter is chronically late for work or else picks a fight with Peter's employer. And he has a few more tricks. I doubt Peter's ever been able to save enough for a deposit on an apartment, especially since Innis makes him pay rent. Any one of us would be willing to help out, but that would mean taking on Innis. Call me a coward; I'd really rather not open *that* Pandora's box."

After a moment, Trey took my hand and murmured, "No, it usually isn't wise to interfere between a parent and a child."

I had the uncomfortable feeling he wasn't just talking about Innis and Peter, but didn't comment.

It was only a little after eight when we joined the others for breakfast. A number of the house party never made an appearance for the meal, and Peter had left the house, so those of us who gathered at the table actually made a fairly congenial group.

Jason was present, and apparently well on his way to reaching a firm friendship with our new stepfather; Adam greeted Trey and me warmly, and won points with me by not mentioning Vanessa, who was absent.

Wanda told me cheerfully that Choo had gotten sick in the middle of the night, but was perfectly all right now and out sunning himself in the garden with Grace—whom he liked. (Wanda had two cats of her own, so she knew very well that the typical feline, overfed or overanxious, upchucks as naturally as you or I cough, after which the problem is usually solved.)

Rounding out the group assembled that morning were Cain and Maddy and Baxter. All were in good moods, and there was even laughter around the table as we ate and talked. The family—or a part of it, anyway—had never seemed so convivial.

HAVE YOU EVER looked back on a troubled period of your life and been able to draw a clean line marking the spot where everything was about to change? Looking back now, I can draw the line right there at breakfast, because a series of events had already been set in motion, and those events led quite logically to what eventually happened.

AFTER BREAKFAST, our congenial little group broke up. Wanda persuaded Jason to go horseback riding with her, and they left. Adam declared, with a twinkle, that he was going to try and get Mother up before her customary time, in which endeavor I wished him luck. Cain and Maddy went out for their usual morning walk; they had taken walks after breakfast for as long as I could remember. Baxter got a cup of coffee for Kerry and took it upstairs, which was a habit of his (and one Kerry loved).

Trey and I left the house; I wanted to show him around, since the dreariness of yesterday had prevented that. We went through the garden, pausing briefly to say good morning to Grace, who was peacefully reading a book in the mild sunlight.

"I think what Grace needs is a long vacation alone. She always looks relaxed without Innis," I remarked as we continued along one of the garden's winding paths.

"The entire family seems more relaxed without Innis," Trey said a bit dryly.

"I know. Maybe he'll do something illegal, and you can arrest him?"

"I'm out of my jurisdiction."

"We don't have to tell him that," I suggested.

"I'd rather not tell the others I'm a cop anyway," Trey said. "Elizabeth and Adam know. You and Jason. The rest of them don't seem to be aware of it, which suits me fine."

I looked up at him as we continued to stroll lazily. "Does it make you uncomfortable? I mean, being known as a cop in a social situation?" The subject had never come up before, and I was honestly curious.

Trey hesitated. "It tends to make those around me uncomfortable. People always expect cops to be looking for crimes, even when we're off duty."

I couldn't help but smile. "You mean you don't?"

He glanced at me, a little wry. "No—at least, not

consciously. But most people feel guilty about something in their lives, and a cop in their midst seems to make guilt stick out all over them.''

''Maybe you just see the guilt *because* you're a cop.''

''It's hard to ignore what you're trained to see,'' he admitted. ''But all the cops I know try to leave the job behind when they're off duty. We need the time away.''

''You brought your gun,'' I observed. Since he had just gotten off duty when we'd left Atlanta, Trey had actually worn his gun (in its accustomed shoulder holster) on the drive out here; it was now in the nightstand drawer beside our bed.

''Habit,'' he explained.

''Well,'' I said, ''if nobody asks, I won't bring up the subject of your job. I have to warn you, though, that Innis is uncanny at finding out things you'd rather he didn't.''

Trey shrugged. ''If he does—so be it. I won't avoid the question if anyone asks.''

Just then, we emerged from the garden and onto the path leading to the stables, so the conversation became more general. The subject lingered in my mind though, because it bothered me. I'm ashamed to admit it, but I hadn't given much thought to how Trey's job affected him—beyond the surface awareness that cops dealt a great deal with pain and suffering.

But I realized then how difficult it must be to probe secret guilts and ask questions no one wants to answer. To have a job it's impossible to leave behind you and forget at the end of the day. What made me the most ashamed was that I *knew* that, knew how painful it was.

I had been forced by circumstance (and prodded by Trey) into just such a situation myself during the Townsend investigation, and I still shied away from the things

I'd felt because of it. So I should have been more sensitive.

Trey dealt with homicide on a daily basis. In many of those cases, it was very much good against evil and almost a pleasure to condemn the clearly guilty villain. But. A large percentage of murders, according to what I'd heard, were impulsive acts. Somebody just got furious, or overcome with some other emotion, and in venting those feelings, killed someone. A crime motivated by anger or frustration or greed, but not by evil. Just ordinary people who were pushed too far—and snapped. A permanent solution for a temporary problem.

I had asked Trey once why he became a cop; he'd replied quite simply that it was because he hated waste. Unfortunately, there is never a neat and tidy resolution to so senseless a crime as murder. Once you begin digging for the truth, waste is all over the place. Wasted lives, wasted energies, wasted emotions.

The unrelenting truth of that must be a heavy burden for any cop, I thought. Because there could never be a clear-cut victory. By the time you emerged from the hunt with a killer caught and condemned, there always seemed to be innocent lives shattered behind you, people changed forever because a murder occurred in their midst.

And ahead for every cop was another killer, and another hunt. How could anyone continue, day after day, looking at the wrecked lives of criminals and victims?

God, how did they stand it? How did Trey stand it? If I finally let down my guard and was able to know him as he really was, how much pain would I find behind the calm, unreadable mask he showed the world?

How many scars? How much unbearable knowledge of the dark side of the human soul?

Does that sound melodramatic? At the time it didn't, because I was facing all those questions for the first time. Now it still doesn't, because I know the answers.

How long do you know a man before you can follow him to his secret places? Soon after Trey and I had met, I'd asked myself that question. Then, my answer to myself had been that it would take years, a lifetime—if ever. But on that mild Saturday, I realized it wasn't a question of time at all. It was a question of the willingness of someone—of me—to meet him halfway. A question of being able to let my own guard down, to trust him and myself to get closer without hurting each other needlessly.

From the beginning, I'd had trouble dividing the man from the cop, thinking, I suppose, that while one could be my lover, the other couldn't. So I'd held back, refusing to admit, even to myself, that what we had was anything other than a casual affair.

It was safe, that. Unthreatening. A pleasurable interlude that would end without pain.

Except that Trey was too complicated, and my feelings for him went too deep, to admit that fiction. If it were only a simple affair, his being a cop wouldn't have troubled me. It wouldn't have mattered. But it did. And for the first time I finally began to understand that Trey was the man he was *because* he was a cop. I couldn't separate him into two people, allowing one into my life while I refused to let the other get close.

Did that simplify our relationship? Hell, no. What it did, really, was to make me aware of the fact that I hadn't been fair to him. Or to the relationship. I couldn't go on thinking of how my reservations about his being a cop affected me without also understanding that they affected him as well.

Our relationship had been wary and tentative, and I had to face the fact that it was my fault. I was being careful because I wasn't comfortable with the cop, and Trey had to follow suit because he knew it was an issue we hadn't dealt with.

Recognition, of course, isn't a solution. And realizing that I'd been wrong didn't mean I would automatically be able to do the right thing from that point on. Problems aren't so easily solved, I'm afraid. But at least it was a start.

As I've mentioned, I'm not a physically demonstrative person, and I'd had trouble touching Trey spontaneously without feeling self-conscious about it. But that morning, as we leaned against a split-rail fence watching Mother's old gray mare grazing contentedly in the pasture, I slipped my hand into Trey's. He turned his head and smiled at me, his fingers closing instantly around mine.

Did I do it because I was feeling ashamed of myself? Maybe. Or maybe I reached out to him because I was feeling a little—more than a little—scared. You see, I'd realized something else. It hadn't come in a blinding flash, and there was still uncertainty in the knowledge, but I had to face it if only inside myself.

Reservations or not, I had turned a corner during the past couple of months, and there was no going back. I had to find a way of dealing with my doubts, because this time I couldn't run, or hide, or pretend the relationship with Trey was a casual thing.

Damn it, I was in love with him.

* * *

IT WAS TYPICAL of me that this new realization made me extremely uneasy. Strong emotions scare me, period. I decided it wasn't something I had to think about just then, and promptly pushed it out of my mind—after silently voicing a number of rational reasons to do that.

Never mind the reasons. None of them made much sense, and all were based on fear.

Anyway, the morning continued. And I thought I managed to act as casual as usual, despite my lack of a poker face. Sheer terror, I expect; some emotions are so powerful they form their own kind of shield.

Trey and I considered playing tennis, but the court was still damp from yesterday's rain, so we decided to wait until afternoon. Since we both loved horses, we ended up spending most of the time outside at the stables and walking through one of the big pastures. I introduced him to my horse, a black Tennessee Walking Horse named Ebony, who was twenty-seven years old and long-retired; he'd been a champion in the show ring when I was in my early teens, and had the excellent disposition and manners of an old gentleman who had been handled gently and treated well for all of his long life.

It's funny. Until I stroked Ebony's velvet nose and told Trey a few childhood stories of long summer rides, I didn't realize how much I missed that part of my life. Like many young girls, I had fallen in love with horses at an early age, riding almost before I could walk and practically living at the stables (to Mother's despair; she rode, but considered it a sport rather than an obsession). But as I'd gotten older, somehow there had been less and less time for horses. Mother's stableman, Reece, had kept my tack clean and in good shape, and tended the horses lovingly, but they were more like pets now.

"Maybe we can go riding tomorrow," I suggested to Trey as I watched Ebony wander away. "I haven't spent a lazy Sunday on horseback in years."

"Sounds good to me," he replied.

"Innis doesn't ride," I said, the prospect growing brighter.

Trey laughed. "That sounds even better. We can pack a picnic lunch, and have a pagan ritual by a stream somewhere."

What woman wouldn't find that plan appealing?

Eventually, we strolled back to the house. Cain and Maddy challenged us to a game of pool, which ended more or less in a draw because Choo jumped up on the table twice and scattered the balls (he likes to play pool). Trey was treated to a few humorous accounts of my childhood from my aunt and uncle, who were, at least, kind enough not to relate some of the more embarrassing and humiliating episodes common to our lives.

Still, I silently cursed family gatherings. I was feeling extremely vulnerable that day, and what I wanted most was a quiet dark corner where I could huddle and think things through. I'm afraid I snapped at Mother at least twice during the morning, which earned me a thoughtful glance from Adam (but no comment, thankfully), and unusual hurt looks from her.

That made me feel like a bitch, which didn't help.

As lunchtime drew near, I felt a bit worried about Peter, who hadn't returned yet, but told myself he was probably enjoying the time away from his father. It was a pity the rest of us couldn't get away—although truly amazing how quickly we found reasons to leave a room moments after Innis entered it. He couldn't find anybody to fight with, even though he tried, because none of us gave him a chance to start.

I heard him yelling at Grace at least once (she'd come into the house and was reading her book in one of the small salons) because she had, apparently, forgotten to pack something he needed. I never did find out what that was.

I barely saw my new stepsister before lunch, which suited me fine. I had gone up to our rooms, leaving Trey involved in a political discussion with Adam and Baxter in the living room, because I wanted to change my shoes. I'd gotten the Reeboks wet during the walk with Trey, and I'm as finicky as a cat when it comes to having wet feet. As I was coming back down, I encountered Vanessa.

I reached the second-floor landing just as she came up from the ground floor. Something had obviously happened. Her cheeks were flaming, her eyes glittering. For a minute, I thought she was about to cry, but as she neared me I got the impression her emotional state was more complicated. She was angry, but excited as well, and peculiarly pleased with herself.

"Vanessa? Is anything wrong?" I'll admit my motive wasn't purely concern for her; the last thing I wanted was some new problem.

She laughed, an oddly shrill sound. "Wrong? No, of course not. I'm just going up to my room for a while. What time is lunch, anyway?"

"It's on the sideboard at twelve-thirty," I answered automatically. "Any time after that is fine." It was nearly eleven at the time.

"Well, I don't want to be disturbed," she said in an irritable tone. "I always rest before lunch."

I could feel my eyebrows climbing, and bit back a remark to the effect that she hadn't done anything during the morning to have earned a need for rest (she hadn't even been up for very long). Instead, I said mildly, "Close your hall door, then. Nobody will bother you."

She gave me a faint smile of acknowledgment (with a clear attitude of noblesse oblige), then sailed on by me.

"You're welcome," I muttered, continuing on my way downstairs. Adam seemed like such a nice man, it was a shame he had such a pain for a kid.

I was returning to the living room, interested in seeing how the political discussion had evolved (in my judgment, you could gauge a man's temper by how well he kept it in a political discussion; Trey and Baxter both could, but I was curious about Adam). I paused in the doorway, though, because I heard Choo grumble the way he does when he's near someone he dislikes.

When I looked back across the entrance hall, I saw my cat coming away from the stairs (the hall was, as I've noted, a large room, but the acoustics were great). Automatically, I looked up to see who had passed him while he was apparently on his way down, and caught a glimpse of Innis going up.

Since I've described Innis and his tastes, you probably know what I was thinking. Vanessa had, after all, been just a bit too concerned with the possibility that her "nap" might be disturbed. And if you're a nice person, you're probably wondering why I didn't immediately rush back upstairs and save her from the consequences of a really lousy decision.

Maybe I should have, because there was no way she could have known what she was getting into. But she *was* over twenty-one, and if she had neither the sense nor the morals to bar a man twice her age from her bedroom when both his wife and her father were in the same house, she deserved whatever she got.

I'm ashamed to admit it, but I felt quite superior to Vanessa as I went on into the living room. I'll also admit that the only thought I had as to consequences was a (pious) wish that both of them keep damned quiet about whatever was going on—at least for the duration of the weekend.

I did *not* want any more problems.

Peter still hadn't returned by lunchtime, but Jason and Wanda came back from their ride with a new friend. They had encountered her a couple of miles away on one of the bridle trails the area was known for (we had a nationally known steeplechase once a year, and there were a dozen riding stables nearby), and had invited her for lunch. Her name was Robin, a girl of about Wanda's age with solemn blue eyes who seemed a little shy and ill-at-ease. She said she was visiting relatives in the area, and had rented a horse to explore the countryside.

She certainly got a bellyful of relatives during lunch that day—and was undoubtedly grateful they weren't hers.

With the exception of Peter, everyone was at the table. As was usual for lunchtime, the sideboard had been set up for a casual meal, with soup and salad, bread and fruit. We served ourselves and sat where we wanted. It was sort of comical how so many of us politely jostled for the chairs farthest from Innis.

The table sat twenty with the two leaves in place—

and they always were. Innis was at one end, and Jason had managed to grab the chair on the opposite end. I sat at Jason's right, and Vanessa had claimed the place on his left (she was wearing a pleased expression but immediately began flirting with Jason; I couldn't tell if she was being discreet or if Innis had failed in an attempted conquest).

On my side of the table, there was me, Trey, Wanda, Robin, Baxter, and Kerry, with three empty chairs between Kerry and Innis. On the other side was Vanessa, Adam, Mother, Cain, Maddy, Lawrence, and Emily, then an empty chair between her and Grace, who was sitting on her husband's right.

Innis never seemed conscious of how most of us avoided sitting near him if we possibly could but, to be honest, it wasn't all that obvious. We were talking and serving ourselves, and it was a casual meal, so maybe it wasn't surprising he didn't feel ostracized.

He barely waited until we were all sitting down before he started. And he started on Mother.

"I liked that Frenchman the best, Elizabeth," he said in that carrying voice of his. The comment came right out of left field, and referred to Mother's fourth husband.

Mother was across the table at an angle from me, but I saw her tense. Adam, on her right, didn't react in any visible way.

With a brief, polite smile directed down the table at Innis, Mother said, "You weren't married to him."

Innis laughed, and I could feel the sound grating on my nerves. "You barely were. What did it last? Six months, seven? And then you ran him off just like the others. We all should have seen which way the wind blew when Daniel left everything he'd known—including two kids and this house—to get away from you.''

Some people are so cruel you can't help wondering if they even belong to the same species as the rest of us. Because when they cut you, it goes straight to the bone.

Mother was very pale, and I felt the strangest mixture of anger and pain. I wanted to yell out something, and I didn't even know what the words would be.

Before I could say anything (and a good thing, too), Jason said very evenly, ''Innis, shut up.''

''Yes,'' Adam agreed, leaning forward slightly to stare down the table with eyes that were suddenly diamond-hard. ''Shut up. At least pretend you know how to be a guest in someone's home.''

Innis flushed an ugly red. ''This isn't your house, Rowland. What right have you—''

''I have the right of any decent human being to throw you out on your ass if you persist in attacking everyone under this roof,'' Adam told him flatly.

I think that was the first moment Innis had an inkling that all of us (with the possible exceptions of Grace and Vanessa) were ranged against him. He looked around the table, meeting a number of very cold or hotly furious eyes, and must have realized that in attacking Mother he'd made a bad mistake. People naturally defend my mother, especially men; I'd noticed that years ago.

There was a very long, very tense silence, and then Mother asked Trey pleasantly if he and I were planning to go riding. It was the only way to really see the countryside, she said.

Trey replied with his usual calm (but with more warmth than usual, so I knew he'd wanted to defend

Mother as well) that we'd decided to ride the following day.

She suggested several trails, Jason contributed his opinion of the best ones, and Wanda chimed in to rule out at least one because it was far too muddy. Tension at our end of the table eased as the conversation continued, all of us trying to ignore the glowering presence of Innis at the other end.

I didn't say very much, I admit. I was still feeling tense. I toyed with my food, having lost my appetite, and looked restlessly around the room. I realized dimly that Innis had begun talking again, but he'd lowered his voice and I didn't pay attention to what he was saying. He must have been addressing his remarks to those nearest him, because I could see that several people were still upset at his end of the table.

He just couldn't seem to learn to keep his mouth shut.

Grace's head was bent, and she looked on the point of tears. When my wandering gaze fell on Emily, she had just sent Innis a look that should have nailed him to his chair. Beside her, Lawrence appeared actually unhappy, which was the first time I'd seen him show any real emotion that I could remember; when he encountered my eyes, he looked hastily away. Even Maddy, usually serene, appeared tense, her lips pressed tightly together as she stared down at her plate. And Cain was pale, his expression curiously fixed.

I thought mine probably was, too. I've commented before that I have my nerves and a couple of other people's as well; when I'm tense or jittery, it takes a while for me to unwind—even given the opportunity. I couldn't wait to get out of that room.

I don't think anyone finished eating. We'd only been

sitting there about half an hour. Which was thirty minutes too long, as far as I was concerned. I finally pushed back my chair and mumbled some vague excuse, and I didn't look back as I left.

FOUR

THE VERANDA was red tile and overlooked both the garden and the area where the cars were parked at one side of the house; it had a number of comfortable patio furnishings—chairs, tables, and lounges. I sat down on one of the lounges, breathing in the fresh air and feeling the mild sunlight slowly warming me. I wondered idly what I would do if, at some future date, Jason married a bitch. Not that I thought he would, but still. Would I be like Mother and suffer the presence of an in-law because I loved my sibling?

Probably.

If that helped explain Innis's presence in the house, it brought no comfort. Damn it, why couldn't we escape family ties that choked us? How could one person as rotten as Innis be allowed to insult everyone around him?

"Montana?" Trey came toward me, a slight frown pulling at his flying brows. "Are you all right?"

One of these days, I'm going to have to cultivate a poker face.

"Yeah, I'm fine," I answered, thinking that if my voice got any more brittle it was going to shatter.

"Would you rather be alone?"

I looked up at him, realizing that he knew me pretty well. When I'm upset about something, my impulse is to retreat and lick my wounds in private, after which I clean maniacally (my loft, Jason's, anything will do) to work through the emotions. I knew that if I said yes, Trey would leave quietly, but I wondered for the first time if it would hurt him.

"No," I said finally, shifting my legs to make room for him to sit on the lounge.

He did, looking at me steadily. "The 'Daniel' Innis was referring to—your father?"

I nodded, avoiding his eyes now. I didn't want to admit, even to him, that Innis's accusation that Mother had driven my father away had upset me so much because it was something I had been thinking since I was ten years old. I didn't want to think about that, much less talk about it. And Trey seemed to sense that.

"Innis knows where to strike, doesn't he?"

"Just like a marksman," I agreed. "Maybe Adam will get fed up and throw him out the front door."

"I suppose your mother invites them for the sake of Grace and Peter?"

"I was sitting here thinking about that. I guess if Jason married someone impossible, I'd put up with her. But Innis is going too far this time, Trey. I've never seen him so bad. If he had *some* redeeming trait, it might be different, but he doesn't. He actually enjoys causing pain."

"At this late stage of his life, he isn't going to change," Trey pointed out. "I've seen his type before."

"God, you mean there's a whole tribe of them?" I said involuntarily.

Trey smiled slightly. "Relatively few—but they do tend to make their presence felt. Try not to let him upset you, Montana."

"I'll try to stay out of his way. But when I can't—make sure there are no sharp objects within reach, okay? I'm not sure I could trust myself."

"I'll do my best," he promised.

I had been vaguely conscious of the sounds of a car, and turned my head then as Peter came up the side steps onto the veranda. He looked unusually cheerful, which made me think that a few months away from his father would make a world of difference in my cousin.

Pausing by the lounge, he said, "Thanks, Trey," and handed over the keys to the Mercedes, adding, "I replaced the gas I used."

"You didn't have to do that," Trey told him.

Peter shrugged, still smiling, and looked at me. "Did I miss lunch?"

"Be thankful you did," I said, sighing. "I imagine there's tons of food left, though."

With undiminished cheerfulness, Peter said, "Good, I'm starved. See you two later."

Watching him disappear into the solarium, I said, "Well, he's certainly in a good mood."

"Think so?" Trey's voice was low.

I looked at him, surprised. "Don't you?"

"I'm not quite sure. He was trying too hard." Trey stared at the keys in his hand, frowning. "That grin of his was about as natural as a mask."

"Better check the Mercedes for dings," I advised, but I wasn't really serious because I was reasonably sure Peter would have said something if he'd wrecked Trey's car. And it was obvious Trey thought the same, because he didn't comment on my remark.

He was silent for a moment, then looked at me. "Maybe it's because I'm an outsider, but I think all of you are underestimating Peter."

"In what way?"

"I think the reasons he puts up with Innis's domination are a lot more complex than weakness. Peter isn't weak, Montana. He's high-strung, and his father's treatment of him keeps him so wound up it's dangerous. If he's pushed too far, he's going to push back."

I had a great deal of faith in Trey's judgment, especially about people, so I couldn't ignore what he said. "Well, if he was putting on a cheerful act just now, I can't think why. It's not something he usually does."

"That's what worries me," Trey said. "Often people appear different when they've made some important decision."

"You mean, maybe he's about to push back?"

"I just don't know him well enough to be sure." Trey hesitated, then said, "I think I'll go talk to him. He's not likely to confide in me, but I may be able to get some idea of his state of mind."

I nodded. "I think I'll stay out here for a while."

With a slight smile, he said, "A little less tense now?"

"A little," I agreed. "Go on, I'm fine. I'm just going to sit here very peacefully and enjoy the sunshine."

And that's what I did, for a while. I was even able to relax a bit more as I sat there listening to the birds and gazing vaguely out over the garden.

Wanda and Robin came out a few minutes later, but just waved as they went on into the garden. I thought they weren't the only ones out there (you could enter the garden from several different directions), but that was one of those absent thoughts you never really connect to anything else. I suppose I caught a glimpse of movement, or heard a voice, but I didn't pay much attention beyond thinking that Grace and Lawrence had both escaped their respective spouses.

Jason came out about ten minutes later, and asked if I wanted to play tennis.

"I'm not in the mood," I replied, eyeing him. "You have the appearance of being a hunted man. Is our new stepsis giving you a hard time?"

Jason almost glared at me, which meant he was feeling pretty rattled; in general, he's even-tempered and not given to emotional outbursts. Tacitly answering the question, he said, "Maybe if I threw out a few hints that I'm gay, she'd leave me alone."

"For a while," I said. "But then she'd probably decide all you need is a good woman to set you straight. Pardon the pun."

"I won't pardon that one," Jason grumbled. "Where's Trey? Maybe he'll give me a game."

"He's in the house, probably talking to Peter." I glanced past my brother and murmured, "Don't look now, but Vanessa's in the solarium."

"I think I'll take a walk," Jason decided promptly, and lost no time in bounding down the steps into the garden.

I had started to add that Innis was also in the solarium, but Jase bolted before I had the chance. Shrugging to myself, I glanced once more toward the house, noted that there was what appeared to be an intimate little discussion going on between Innis and Vanessa, and then returned my attention to the garden.

My reverie was disturbed again about five minutes later when Wanda climbed up the steps alone.

"Where's your friend?" I asked.

"Oh, she had to go. I offered to ride back with her, but she said no thanks. I think Innis made her uncomfortable, Lane—she couldn't wait to leave."

"I don't blame her."

"No, me either. He's really being nasty this weekend, isn't he?"

"Blue-ribbon nasty."

Shrugging off the subject, Wanda eyed me hopefully. "Do you want to play tennis? The court's dry now."

"Jason was looking for a partner a few minutes ago; why don't you ask him?"

"Where is he?"

"He was in the garden. If you didn't see him out there, I don't know where he is."

"I could yell, but that isn't dignified," she decided. "I think I'll go lean on his car horn."

"That's dignified?" I asked with a laugh.

"No, but I bet he'll come running. Men are so peculiar about their cars, don't you think? Every car parked out there is a different model, so all the horns sound just a little different; I bet you a dollar Jason will recognize the sound of his Cougar, and that he'll be the only one to come when it calls."

"You're on," I said, amused and a bit curious. Wanda winked at me and headed for the cars, and I sat there, alone again, as I waited for the sound of a car horn.

My thoughts were, however, on the irony of my expectations of this weekend. Even though I'd tried to stop thinking about it, Wanda had brought up Innis's name and reminded me. I'd expected the tension between me and Mother, but hadn't given much thought to the other members of my family.

Frowning to myself, I caught a brief snatch of an

argument somewhere nearby but, before I could try to identify the voices, Wanda leaned on the horn of Jason's car. I found out then that the acoustics out there were definitely weird. The sound of the horn bounced around, and I could have sworn I heard a female voice cry out, "How could you?" without the faintest idea of which direction it had come from.

I looked toward the house, but didn't see anyone in the solarium, and all I heard after the car horn died away was a couple of irritated cheeps from the birds.

Jason appeared, coming up the steps from the garden to demand, "Who's blowing my horn?"

"Wanda," I replied. "And I think I owe her a dollar. Jase, who's in the garden?"

"I didn't see anybody. Why?"

"I thought I heard somebody fighting. Not that it's so surprising, I suppose."

"Not this weekend, it isn't." He looked past me as Wanda returned to the veranda, and asked her, "What's the big deal?"

"I want to play tennis, and Lane said you were looking for a partner."

"Great," he said. "Lanie?"

I decided the veranda wasn't such a peaceful place after all, and abandoned it with a sigh. "Okay, if Trey's ready for a game, we'll play against you two. If not, I'll watch."

"You owe me a dollar," Wanda reminded.

TREY AND I didn't get much of a chance to talk privately for the rest of the day, since we kept pretty busy. By the time we went to our room, there wasn't a whole lot of time to dress for dinner.

I was ready first, for two reasons: because I hardly

wear makeup (the absolute minimum), and because Trey decided he needed to shave. While he was occupied in the bathroom, I wandered out into the sitting room putting on my earrings and muttering curses because of my shoes. Given the fact that I live in Reeboks (I've tried other brands, but, if you ask me, no other compares), dress shoes are pure torture.

Unfortunately, Mother demanded that we dress for dinner. Not black tie, but a long way from my usual jeans or sweatsuits. And since it was her roof, I did my best to obey her rules. So I was wearing a simple green ''cocktail'' dress, pantyhose (which I despise; I decided I'd try garters one day soon and see how Trey reacted), and moderate heels. Jewelry consisted of my everyday watch (black leather band and a cat on the face, with a mouse circling as the second hand), a thin gold chain at my neck, and small diamond earrings.

The earrings were as big a pain as the heels. I stood at the Palladian window looking out absently as I struggled with the tiny little backs jewelry makers persistently torment us with.

It was raining, which didn't really surprise me. From early spring until late fall, weather in the South can be really weird. I just hoped it would clear by morning. A nice long horseback ride with Trey sounded perfect for Sunday.

My eye caught a glimpse of movement outside, and I stepped closer to the window to see who was walking around out there getting wet. The uncovered blond hair identified her to me immediately; Maddy loved walking in the rain, and never wore a hat or scarf. I would have opened the window and leaned out to yell down at her, except that the damned Palladian window in this room didn't open.

Watching as she moved gracefully across the driveway (she must have gone down to visit the stables), I was mildly surprised to see that she wasn't the only houseguest out in the rain. I was even more surprised when I realized the other one was Innis.

I couldn't tell what he'd been doing out there; he was coming from the general area where the cars were parked at the side of the house. Knowing him, he'd probably been checking to make sure his precious baby (a classic Thunderbird) wasn't getting its fenders wet.

I was no more than mildly interested to see that when he and Maddy met a few yards away from the steps, they stopped and appeared to be talking. I couldn't read their expressions, so I had no warning at all before Maddy slapped him.

After the instant of shock, my first emotion was wry amusement. I'd discovered years ago that Innis had an eye for pretty blonds (actually, women in general, but he favored blonds), and it didn't surprise me very much that—even with Vanessa apparently on his string—he might have made a verbal pass at Maddy. The fact that she was a relative by marriage wouldn't have stopped him. (I knew that, because he'd made a few suggestive remarks to me during my early twenties.)

Of course, he might simply have insulted her, which was about as likely—but that slap had been awfully quick, like a gut reaction to something immensely distasteful.

Though I couldn't see his face very well because of the distance and angle, it was obvious that Innis was more amused than upset about the slap. I could have sworn he was laughing. It looked like he said something else to her, then turned and strolled away—toward the side of the house rather than the front door.

Maddy stood there for a full minute before she took a few steps toward the house. Then she went very still. My amusement faded as I watched her; I had the kind of peculiar feeling you get when you're watching a suspenseful movie and the changing tempo of the music warns you that something awful is about to happen.

I craned to look straight down, and saw Cain. He was standing on the steps, as still as Maddy. After a long time, she continued toward him, and they disappeared from my view.

I stood by the window for a while longer, watching the rain. Not thinking very much. I didn't move until Trey was ready to go downstairs.

AT FIRST, the evening seemed a virtual repeat of the previous one. We gathered in the living room, as usual, for drinks. All of us were a bit restless, moving around the room more than we had the evening before, with loose groups forming, drifting apart, and then reforming. Innis was, surprisingly, less belligerent than usual, and Peter still wore his cheerful mask.

It *was* a mask, I could see that now. Peter smiled too widely, talked too rapidly, and stayed as far away from his father as possible. He was even polite to Jason.

"What's with him?" Jase asked me in a low voice a few minutes before dinner was to be announced. "He actually asked me if I take commissions for portraits."

"It is weird, isn't it?" I kept my voice low as well, so that only Trey and Jason heard me. "You know, I could swear he was scared."

Trey frowned slightly. "Scared?"

"Well, it's just an impression. But I remember years ago when we were all spending Christmas here. Peter sneaked out one night, and the next day he acted something like he is now. It turned out that he'd borrowed his father's car and gotten a speeding ticket, and he was scared Innis would find out.''

''Yeah, I remember that,'' Jason said. ''But if this is the same kind of thing—what the hell's he done?''

''God knows,'' I said.

And, at that apt moment, it happened.

''Larry?'' Emily's voice was high and shrill, cutting through every other conversation in the room. She was sitting on a loveseat beside Lawrence, and was half turned toward him, one of her plump hands patting his shoulder frantically. ''Larry, what is it? What's wrong?''

We were all staring, the room silent except for her voice. His head was bowed, and I couldn't see his face because of the angle, but I heard a dull thud and numbly watched a glass roll across the rug and come to rest against Innis's shoe. Automatically, he started to bend down and get it, but Trey's voice stopped him cold.

''No, don't touch it.''

I think I knew even before Trey spoke. I think I knew when Emily cried out Lawrence's name the way she had. I felt very chilled as I watched Trey cross the room and bend over the loveseat.

He tilted Lawrence's head back against the cushion, and we could all see the slack face that was a peculiar color, and the half-opened eyes. I don't suppose Trey had to check the carotid pulse, but he did, a frown pulling at his brows, and then he looked across the room straight at me and shook his head slightly. He was still frowning, and even from that distance I could see a too-familiar hard expression in his luminous gray eyes. His cop's eyes.

Oh, hell, no, I thought numbly.

"No, he's not," Emily said, staring at Trey with huge eyes and a hectic flush on her cheeks. "He can't be. Not my Larry. Larry, honey—" She began patting his shoulder again, with so much force this time that we could all hear it.

I guess for a couple of minutes there, we all looked like waxwork figures. It was the shock of a death, naturally, but it was also, I think, the shock of who had died. It was the first time Lawrence had ever caused a commotion.

Trey glanced over at Mother, who started slightly and immediately came toward him, then pulled Emily up from the loveseat, being as gentle as possible. He sort of handed her to Mother. She was sobbing by then, rough, ugly sounds, and kept muttering, "Not my Larry," over and over again.

I saw Trey shake out his handkerchief and bend to pick up Lawrence's glass. He held it for a moment, studying whatever was left inside, and an even colder feeling swept through me as I realized what he was doing. There was something in the glass, something that shouldn't have been there.

I had already known; Trey's eyes had told me. But I didn't want to believe it. As if from a great distance, I heard Innis speak in a hoarse voice.

"We should call a doctor."

"No," Trey said quietly, setting the glass on the small table beside the loveseat. "We should call the police."

"Why?" Innis demanded, but he was eyeing the glass Trey had picked up, and his face was pale.

When Trey replied to the question, he was gazing across the room at me. "Because it looks like poison."

Again, it was Innis who spoke, his voice even harsher. "How do you know that?"

I heard my own voice then, and it was so amazingly calm I must have been in shock. "Trey's a police officer," I said, then looked Innis in the eye and added flatly, "Homicide."

In a way, the shock of my announcement was as great as Lawrence's death, at least to some of the people present. In the momentary silence that followed it, I looked around the room, feeling numb and not thinking very much.

They really did look like waxworks, pale and staring, their faces curiously unfamiliar to me.

Peter was peering at Lawrence with the most peculiar expression, almost as if he wanted to laugh wildly, and I didn't know if he'd even heard me. Cain took two steps away from the bar to stand beside Maddy's chair, both of them white but calm; they were gazing at Trey with expressions I couldn't read. Mother was holding Emily, who was still sobbing and looking (if she could see at all through the streaming tears) back and forth between Lawrence and Trey. I don't know what Mother was thinking; her face was pale and completely blank.

Adam effectively hid whatever he felt. Vanessa looked shocked and somewhat disbelieving, as if death were a personal affront and a cop in the house was even worse. Jason was frowning, his gaze moving around the room from person to person; after the Townsend murder, both my brother and I knew more than we wanted to about the effects of a death—especially if that death turned out to be murder.

God, let it be an accident, I thought.

Grace was sitting bolt upright in her chair, her wide

eyes fixed on Lawrence's body as if it were something obscene, and I got the feeling she hadn't heard anything that had been said. Shock, I supposed. Wanda, white to the lips and silent, had gone instinctively to be with her parents, and all of them were looking at Trey rather dazedly. Innis was looking at Trey as well, but his sensual features were twisted in distaste.

"A cop," he muttered.

Trey ignored that. His own face was grim, but his voice remained calm when he said, "I think we should all move to another room. Leave your glasses here, please."

"Why?" Innis demanded fiercely.

Trey turned to stare at him, and right then he was every inch a cop with years of experience, responsibility, and command at his back. "Because, until the proper authorities arrive, I'm considering this a potential crime scene—and acting accordingly. Now, put your glass down and leave the room."

I wasn't very surprised that Innis, after an instant of rigid silence, scowled and put his glass on the mantel behind him. Around the room, the rest of us were following suit, more or less automatically. There are some tones of voice which not only do not invite question, but also trigger the instinct to obey whoever is clearly in charge.

Trey was.

Alexander appeared just then in the doorway, his expression as calm and detached as always. He knew what had happened. He always knew what went on in the house. He didn't glance toward Lawrence, but looked across the room directly at Trey. "Shall I call the police, sir?"

"No, I will. Settle everyone in another room, will

you, please, Alexander? The parlor across the hall will be fine. And it would help if you could round up all the staff and have them ready; they'll have to give statements.''

''Yes, sir.''

I was deliberately the last out of the room, and waited in the doorway until Trey joined me. With very little hope, I asked, ''Could it have been an accident?''

Trey looked past me at the group slowly retreating across the hall (only Emily was making a sound), then gazed at me with very hard cop's eyes. ''You mean, could he have eaten bad mushrooms for lunch, or chewed on a sprig of belladonna out in the garden?''

If that sounded sarcastic, it wasn't. His low voice, strained and rougher than I'd ever heard it, gave him away. I had the sudden intuition that he wanted to put his arms around me, but that he couldn't. He couldn't, not because he was a cop, but because right now he was a cop to *me*—and both of us knew it.

It seemed that my reservations about him being a police officer were threatening to come between us for a second time. The worst part was that I couldn't help how I felt, and I couldn't hide my feelings. I'm not very good at that. At that moment, I wished I was.

Because somebody had to say it, I did. ''So it's murder?''

''I'm sorry, Montana,'' Trey said. ''I don't see any other answer. Arsenic, I think.''

There were dozens of questions in my head, but I couldn't ask any of them right then. I could literally feel myself drawing inward, trying to retreat from the pain I could see lying ahead. Someone in the house was a killer, and I knew only too well what that would do to all of us.

I wanted to reach out to Trey, but I couldn't. Without another word, I turned and followed the others.

I KNOW. I was being unfair to Trey again. He certainly hadn't asked for what was happening, and it was natural that he would take charge of the situation. Murder was, after all, one of the things he knew best. But, like I've said, hiding your head in the sand is a perfect invitation to be blindsided, and I was reeling a bit from the impact.

If you don't know what I'm talking about, I'll put it as briefly as possible. Murder investigations are messy and painful. To Trey, they are necessary, and he happens to be good at them; to me . . . well, let's just say I'd much, *much* rather not get involved. I tend to run from things that hurt.

Unfortunately, I doubted that I'd be able to run from this. Trey was here. I loved him—and he was a cop. I wished he wasn't a cop. More than anything, I wished that.

Not an excuse. Just an explanation.

So I rejoined my family, trying very hard to detach myself from the situation. Calm and neutral, that was the ticket. After all, it *was* possible that Lawrence's death had been a bizarre accident. And, if it hadn't been, then it could have been suicide (though, with the exception of jumping off a building during rush hour or going berserk with a rifle and taking a few of your fellow humans with you, suicide tended to be a rather private matter that did not take place in a crowd of people). Or a nameless stranger could have popped into the house, unnoticed by more than twenty people, and made himself invisible long enough to slip rat poison into Lawrence's drink.

Sure.

In the parlor, the family arranged itself silently around the room, and I felt very lonely for a few minutes. Not sharing Innis's thick-skinned nature, I knew only too well that the majority of my family was avoiding sitting near me. Some of the glances I got were wary and almost betrayed, and I understood then what Trey had meant about the effect of a cop's presence on people.

Damn it, almost all of them looked guilty! They wore closed, secret faces, and looked at me with shuttered eyes. Obviously, at least some of them had an inkling of some of the questions to come, and nobody was happy at the prospect.

No one commented at first. Mother sent Alexander to check with Trey, and then she and Kerry took Emily—who was clearly hysterical—upstairs. Mother said she was going to call a doctor friend of hers in Atlanta, and have him come out to the house for Emily's sake, and I think all of us silently agreed she needed to be sedated.

When they were gone, it was, of course, Innis who made the first remark. And I guess I should have expected him to attack me.

"Why the hell didn't you tell us he was a cop?" he demanded, scowling at me.

I was sitting in a chair near the door, trying to keep my mind blank and not having very much luck. "It didn't seem important," I answered.

"No? Well, if your boyfriend's right and it is poison, it's obvious he doesn't think it was an accident. That means he believes somebody slipped Lawrence a fatal mickey. You think that would have happened if every-

one had known there was a cop watching every move
we made?''

"Shut up, Innis,'' Jason ordered brusquely, coming
away from the window where he'd been standing to sit
down on the arm of my chair.

I was grateful for the support. Because, damn him,
Innis could have been right. I mean, would *you* murder
somebody with a cop in the house? Especially a homicide detective? Could Trey and I have prevented a
death if we'd only mentioned he happened to be a police officer?

There's a thought to haunt you.

"Don't tear at yourself," Jason said to me quietly.
"You couldn't have known. And it might not have made
a difference anyway.''

I can't say I felt very reassured; on that point, I never
have been. It might not have made a difference, true.
But it also might have. Still, I had to accept the fact
that hindsight wasn't going to change what had happened; it never does. Trying not to think about it, I
said, "Why Lawrence? That's what I don't get. Nobody
hated Lawrence.''

"It could have been an accident," Jason offered.

I should have kept my mouth shut (I doubted Trey
would want all my relatives to know the information),
but I replied to that without considering. "It's a little
hard to take rat poison by accident.''

Shocked, Wanda said, "Rat poison?''

I looked around the room to find everyone staring at
me, and wished I had kept quiet. It was a little late by
then, however. Reluctantly, I said, "Trey thinks it might
have been arsenic, and you sometimes find that in rat
poison.''

"Any other tidbits you'd like to share with us?" Innis asked sardonically.

"Not at the moment." I kept my voice even, but it took a hell of an effort.

Musingly—and with an ugly little smile—Innis said, "I wonder how many of us knew that rat poison contains arsenic. I certainly didn't."

Jason glared at him. "What're you trying to do—implicate Lane? Well, if knowledge counts—include me. Like a lot of people, I read labels. I've also read a few murder mysteries in my time. But I didn't have anything against Lawrence, and neither did Lanie."

"None of us did," Baxter said, frowning.

"One of us obviously did," Innis pointed out.

"It had to be somebody from outside," Wanda said, looking at me with anxious eyes. "Somebody we don't know. It could have been, couldn't it, Lane?"

I had to answer the appeal, though I didn't like the answer. "Sorry, sweetie, but that isn't very likely. The only stranger who's been here in the house this weekend was Robin, and she left hours ago. We would have noticed somebody else. Besides, if the poison was in Lawrence's glass—it had to have been put there by one of us in the room. I don't see how it could have been done beforehand."

"You think it was his drink?" Jason asked, looking down at me.

"I fixed his drink," Cain said flatly, also looking at me. "As usual."

I felt a little chill, and spoke hastily to ward off unthinkable possibilities. "We were all moving around in the room, and all of us set our glasses down from time to time. We usually do that. Any one of us could have slipped something into Lawrence's glass and moved away without drawing attention to the action.'' My mind was already furiously debating that point when Jason spoke.

"Yeah, maybe, but wouldn't Lawrence have noticed his drink tasted a little strange? I mean, enough rat poison to kill him so quickly—if that's what it was— must have changed the flavor of his scotch.''

The wording might have been flippant—Jason's way of handling discomfort—but the point was valid. I nodded. "You'd think. And there should have been some sign that he was ill or in pain before he died, or so I would have thought.'' I looked around the room at those closed faces. "Did anybody notice anything odd about him?''

Wryly, Jason said, "I don't remember even looking at him until Emily cried out. I know I didn't speak to him. Even now . . . I couldn't tell you the color of his tie.''

There was a short silence, all of us, I think, realizing that we hadn't noticed Lawrence at all. I couldn't have described what he had been wearing either, damn it— and I'd been (supposedly) trained to automatically take note of that kind of detail.

Some investigator I was.

Suddenly, jarringly, Peter laughed. He was sitting in a chair near one corner of the room, and when I looked at him I felt very uneasy. His eyes were bright, a flush reddened his pale cheeks, and he appeared feverishly wound up.

"Poor Lawrence,'' he said in a thin voice, an odd little smile curving his lips. "The only time the family ever notices him is when he drops dead—and then only after Emily draws our attention to him.''

"We're all upset," Grace murmured, looking at her son worriedly.

Innis let out a snort at that lame comment, but then fell silent. Like the rest of us, he didn't seem to have anything else to say.

I wished I could turn my mind off, but that was impossible. Even as conscious as I was of the likely pain ahead for all of us, and my building anxiety, I couldn't help worrying the puzzle. There was too much that didn't make sense, beginning with who had died.

Lawrence? What on earth had that mild, almost invisible man done to make somebody want to kill him? It seemed more absurd than tragic, as if someone had made an embarrassing mistake. So sorry, my aim was off—I didn't mean for *you* to down the poison, old bean.

Even now, we were all more concerned with the mystery of what had happened and how it had happened rather than who it had happened *to*. Poor Lawrence wasn't even being noticeably mourned, except by his wife.

And what about the points Jason had made? Could anybody drink down an arsenic tonic without at least wondering why his scotch tasted funny? Granted, Lawrence was—had been—the kind of man who pretty much ate and drank what was put in front of him without comment, but surely he would have given at least some sign that he was dying of poison?

At least said "pardon me" or something?

Like everything else that I knew about him, his death had been so . . . imperceptible. Not with a bang *or* a whimper, but more like a sigh.

So I sat there, chewing on my thumbnail, surrounded by relatives—one of whom might well be a killer—and tried to make some sense out of it.

The room had been silent for quite a while when we heard the arrival of the police, and I could feel even more tension seep into the room. I don't know how many of the others were aware of it, but both Jase and I knew we'd be dealing with county cops; we were outside both Atlanta and the surrounding area of Fulton County, and not near a particular town.

This was, in general, a very quiet area, with scattered homes, stables, and bridle paths. I couldn't recall there having been a murder. It was very likely that, of the cops presently in the house, Trey was the only one with experience in investigating a murder.

Great.

Obviously thinking along the same lines, Jason leaned down a bit and murmured, "It'll be Trey, won't it?"

I kept my voice low as well. "That depends on the county cops. If their ranking officer asks for his help . . ."

"Lanie . . . don't let it bust you two up."

My brother knows me very well, and he knows Trey better than Trey realizes, so his remark wasn't an idle one.

I wanted to say that I didn't know if I could handle this. That I felt scared and miserable, and wanted to run. But I didn't say any of that. I just continued to chew on my thumbnail and tried not to listen to the sounds of voices and activity coming from that room across the hall.

FIVE

Trey appeared in the doorway about an hour later, and looked at me, expressionless. "Lane?"

I got up from my chair and went to him, thinking vaguely that he only called me Lane when there were other people around (if it was just Jason, he usually called me Montana).

When I reached him, Trey looked at the others and spoke matter-of-factly. "An officer will begin taking your statements in a few minutes. You'll be called out of this room, one by one, and asked to detail your movements since this morning. After that, you're free to go upstairs or wherever you like. But don't leave the grounds without notifying an officer."

Innis probably would have had something to say about that, but Trey didn't give him the chance to utter a word. He took my arm and led me out into the entrance hall, where a uniformed officer waited.

"Lane, this is Captain Nick Winslow. County police."

"Captain." He was about Trey's age (thirty-five) and height (six two), and had the polished appearance I've noticed is fairly common among county police; his uniform was extremely neat and well-pressed, and everything that could seemed to gleam with meticulous care—from his badge to his black shoes. When he spoke, he had a much stronger accent than either Trey or I, which made me think he was probably from one of the small towns in that part of the state.

"Miss Montana. I want to say right off that I value Trey's opinion—and he seems pretty damned sure you wouldn't drown a week-old kitten."

I winced at the analogy (as any genuine cat person would), then looked up at Trey as it reminded me of something. "Where's Choo?"

"I haven't seen him," Trey replied.

"Choo?" Winslow looked somewhat puzzled.

"My cat," I explained. "He's around here somewhere. Supposed to be, I mean." Then the point of Winslow's statement sunk in, and I looked at each of the two men dwarfing me. "You two know each other?"

"We were rookies together in Atlanta too many years ago," Trey said.

Winslow caught up with the conversation (he had considerably less experience than Trey in following my thoughts, and the side issue of Choo had obviously thrown him momentarily) to say, "I decided Atlanta Metro wasn't the place for me, and ended up out here."

That information was somewhat cheering, though I admit it hardly made a dent in my growing tension. Still, I thought it was a good bet that the investigation of Lawrence's death wouldn't be quite as by-the-book as it would have been in Atlanta, given both Winslow's laid-back air and his clear willingness to trust Trey's word. That was good.

"Funny," I commented, referring back to Winslow's

analogy. "I didn't even think about being a suspect myself."

"Too concerned about everyone else?" Trey asked.

I shrugged, looking at Winslow. "So you are treating this as a homicide?"

"I pretty much have to," he said with a faintly unhappy look. "Myself, I probably would have thought Mr. Stoddard had died of a heart attack, but Trey knows better than me what to look for, and he says it's poison. There was sediment in the glass right enough, and the corpse—uh, Mr. Stoddard's body—shows signs of poison. Until somebody convinces me different, I'm ruling out suicide or accident."

He glanced at Trey, his spaniel-brown eyes hesitant, then added, "I've officially asked Trey to assist in the investigation, since it's more his line and since he's been here in the house. He seems to think I couldn't go wrong in asking for your help as well."

Just between you and me, Captain Nick Winslow *almost* had me fooled. Almost. He had his act down pat, all nice and "Aw, shucks, ma'am," a good ole boy from the country with a guileless face and naive eyes.

But I didn't buy it. First, if he'd been a rookie in Atlanta, innocent he wasn't. Second, Trey doesn't suffer fools gladly, and I was positive these two were friends rather than merely past acquaintances, because it showed. And, third, it is never a good idea to underestimate a cop; very few of them become cops just because there's nothing better to do.

I wondered if Trey thought I was fooled, but decided to wait and see on that score. Instead, I replied to Winslow's remarks quite mildly. "I see. I have to tell you, Captain, I'm not very comfortable with the idea. Unless we can conjure a stranger out of thin air, I'm likely to find myself related to a murderer. Not a happy thought.''

Winslow nodded in complete understanding. "I can see how you'd feel that way, Miss Montana. Still, if we don't get to the bottom of things, there'll be hell to pay. Wouldn't you rather know the truth—however it turns out?''

"I guess I should, shouldn't I?" I sighed, telling myself over and over that I couldn't blame Trey for this. But I still felt miserable and more than a little scared. "When will we know for sure if it was poison?"

"The body's on its way to Atlanta now," Winslow told me. "We don't have the facilities for an autopsy around here. Since this is Saturday night, and since the Fulton County M.E. has a heavy workload, Trey thinks it'll be Monday at the earliest before we get confirmation.''

"And we're all under house arrest in the meantime?''

Winslow looked hurt. "I need everybody to stay in the area, that's all. Way I understand it, most of these folks live outside the state.''

Trey said, "The sooner we get at the truth, the sooner everyone can go home.''

I knew he meant the two of us as much as the others, but I didn't comment or look at him. Instead, I kept my eyes on Winslow. "Then I guess I haven't got much of a choice. How can I help, Captain?''

I felt Trey move slightly beside me, the way you shift your weight when something's bothering you, and I was vaguely surprised that he'd given himself away. He didn't, usually, not with body language. But I suppose he'd heard something in my voice. He knew I was angry, and he probably thought I blamed him for the sit-

uation. I didn't. But I blamed him for being a cop,
damn it, for being willing to use me because I could
be a tool to help him find the truth.

I'd known he would.

From the moment I realized Lawrence hadn't died a
natural death, I had known he'd pull me into this. Pull
me over the line to his side. The problem was, my
family was on the other side of that line.

So, yeah, I was mad. And I was hurting. Once before, he'd made me feel like a Judas. But this time was
worse. This was my family—and Trey was the man I
loved.

Winslow glanced between us with a slightly uncertain expression; I knew damned well he felt the tension,
and since I have zero chance of hiding my feelings, it
was a safe bet he knew I was angry—even if he wasn't
sure why. Right then, however, I didn't particularly care
what he thought. I just wanted to get through this as
quickly as possible, and I was praying that somebody
else would be the one to figure out who in the house
was a murderer.

And praying that no one I cared about would turn
out to be that killer.

Clearing his throat, Winslow said, "We, uh, we'd
like you to take a look at the living room. Trey's told
me what he recalls of the movements of everyone involved, and we've come up with a notion of what might
have happened. If you spot the same thing, that'll help
give it weight."

I didn't have the foggiest idea what he meant, and
felt uncomfortably like a guinea pig. So—they had a
theory, and wanted to see if I could walk in cold and
spot it? Great, that was great.

"I'm not a detective," I pointed out to Winslow. "I find lost things, that's all."

"Yes, ma'am, I know. But I understand you're quite observant, and you know your family."

I don't know about you, but there's just something about being called ma'am by a man with a southern accent that makes me feel I should curtsy. And that's not an extraneous observation, either; Winslow's act was very beguiling.

I mentally shook off the feeling, nodded to show I was willing to give it a shot, and walked with them across the remainder of the hall to the living room.

The body had, thankfully, been removed. Other than that, the room didn't seem any different. There were a couple of uniformed officers standing near the door, one with a clipboard, and both of them looked at me the way cops do—with an intent, measuring stare.

I ignored them, and instinctively went to the place where I'd been standing when Emily had cried out; it was near the bar, beside it actually. My glass was still there, along with Trey's, Jason's, and Cain's.

Neither Trey nor Winslow said anything, or offered any further direction, and for a couple of minutes I felt very self-conscious and uncertain. I stood there, looking slowly around the room, and flashes of memory began to pop up in my head. Without really being aware of it, I spoke out loud.

"Just before Emily cried out, Trey and I were here, along with my brother and uncle; these are our glasses. The three of us were standing right here at this end of the bar, but Cain was at the other end, near his wife. Maddy was sitting in that chair; she usually does. Her glass is on the table beside it. And—Peter's glass, too. He was standing near her. Baxter and Kerry were on the couch, so the glasses on this side of the coffee table must be theirs. On the other side of the coffee table—that couch—it was Vanessa and Adam; Mother was leaning against the back of the couch close to him and talking to Grace. She was in that chair near the fireplace, and she wasn't drinking; she never does. Wanda—where was Wanda? She was . . . Oh—at this end of the room. She'd just said something to Peter, and then turned as if she was about to come toward us.

"Emily and Lawrence were on the loveseat. Emily's glass is on the little table on this side of it—and you've put Lawrence's on the other table between the loveseat and the fireplace, which is where he set it when it wasn't in his hand. No, that has to be a duplicate glass—isn't it?"

"A duplicate," Winslow confirmed. "His is on its way to the lab."

I nodded a vague acknowledgment, then went on remembering. "Innis was standing at the fireplace, like he always does, and his glass is on the mantel."

I was aware that the officer with the clipboard was silently making notes, but then something began to nag at me. There was a wrongness. Something about—the glasses? Frowning, I thought about it.

As a group, we'd been casual with our drinks, putting them down and picking them up several times. Nobody held their drinks in their hands all the time, as far as I could remember. With all the little tables scattered about, there were innumerable places in the room where a glass could be set down . . .

My gaze focused on Innis's glass. That wasn't right. Why wasn't it right?

I walked slowly across the room, stopping a couple of feet away from the place where Lawrence had died.

His glass—the duplicate glass—had been placed on the table that had been between him and Innis, with a crystal coaster neatly underneath it. Yeah, that was right, that was where he would have set his glass when he wasn't drinking from it. And the coaster made me even more sure; I was certain that if there hadn't been a coaster, Lawrence would have held his glass constantly rather than set it down anywhere. It wasn't nice to leave water rings on other people's furniture, and Lawrence was—nobody would ever deny it—a very thoughtful and considerate guest.

I took another step and reached down, brushing my index finger across the table inches behind Lawrence's glass. Dampness. Somebody had put a glass down on the table and left it long enough to produce a water ring. Trey had put Lawrence's empty glass on the table earlier, but he'd set it at the front of the table beside the coaster—and it had been wrapped in his handkerchief. The water ring was definitely inches away, behind the coaster. The exact area where someone standing near the fireplace would have absently set a glass.

I looked up at the mantel, at Innis's glass, then looked at the table again where Lawrence's rested in the coaster. They were identical. And even though he had put his glass on the mantel before leaving the room, it was very likely that Innis had, at some point, used the table for the same purpose. Especially since the mantel was too high to provide a casual resting place for anyone's glass, and since Innis didn't give a damn about water rings on other people's furniture.

I should say here that Cain had a longstanding habit whenever he played bartender. He put certain drinks in certain glasses. Brandy always went into a snifter, wine into goblets, sweet drinks into tall, thin glasses—and so on. He always put scotch in short crystal tumblers with a heavy leaded design on the base. Trey had been given one such glass, since he'd asked for scotch, and his was on the bar across the room.

Only two other people had like glasses.

My thoughts weren't happy ones. I couldn't think of a single reason why anyone would have murdered Lawrence—but motives were everywhere if Innis had been the intended target.

"Damn," I muttered, forgetting about my silent audience. "It could have been meant for Innis. The glasses could have been switched by mistake after the poison was in; Lawrence wouldn't have said anything if Innis had picked up his glass. He probably wouldn't have even noticed."

Startling me, Winslow chuckled and said, "Trey thought you'd spot it."

I turned to stare at them, feeling more afraid than I'd been at any point until then. "That's what you hoped I'd see? That somebody could have tried to poison Innis and gotten Lawrence by mistake?"

Winslow came farther into the room and leaned against the back of a chair, gazing at me intently. "Well, judging by what Trey's told me, Mr. Stoddard doesn't seem to have had an enemy in the house. Mr. Langdon, however, seems to make a habit of getting on people's nerves. Can you think of a reason why anybody'd want to kill Mr. Stoddard?"

"No," I said slowly.

"How about Mr. Langdon? Would it have surprised you very much if it had been him killed?"

"No, it wouldn't have surprised me," I admitted reluctantly, hearing the hollow note in my voice. Dear God, I'd said as much to Trey.

Trey spoke up then, his voice quiet. "Identical glasses and drinks, within reach of both men. All of us moved around the room quite a bit. I know I saw Innis turn away at least a couple of times—and there were two glasses on the table. Anyone could have slipped something into one of the glasses, believing it was Innis's drink."

Even more reluctantly, I said, "I don't think any of us except Emily looked at Lawrence without reason. We just didn't notice him. But whenever Innis moves, you can't help but watch him. He's like a snake or an unfriendly dog; you want to keep your eyes on him."

"So," Winslow said, "if Mr. Langdon moved, you'd all be watching him? And maybe you wouldn't see somebody else doctor that drink beside Mr. Stoddard?"

"That's a big maybe," I said, but couldn't think of anything better. "Okay, it could have happened that way—but I'm having a hard time believing more than a dozen people missed it, especially since one of them was a homicide detective."

"Thanks a lot," Trey murmured.

I didn't look at him, or apologize for the snide remark. I should have, but I didn't. Instead, I kept right on talking to Winslow. "And I just don't see how Lawrence could have drunk scotch laced with enough poison to kill him apparently without tasting it, or how he could have died so quickly and quietly. Wouldn't he have gotten sick first? Been in pain? Wouldn't there have been some sign he'd been poisoned?"

You may notice that I was still trying very hard to deny a murder had taken place.

Winslow glanced at Trey, who replied in a very stolid voice. "Different poisons cause different reactions in the body, but like everything else in life, there's no absolute answer. People vary in their reactions. If it was arsenic, Lawrence should have been in pain and felt ill—but he could also have had a high tolerance for pain, and he could have believed it was nothing more than an upset stomach."

"While he was dying?" I demanded skeptically.

"It's possible, Montana."

We were staring at each other by now, and though Trey's face was expressionless I knew mine was, to say the least, tense. Winslow broke into the silence in a very mild tone—the kind a man uses when he feels the need to tread warily.

"My men are taking statements from the others, and I've instructed them to just ask the basic questions of where everybody was and what they did today. All the bedrooms have been searched just to play it safe; we didn't find anything out of place and no poison, not surprisingly. Given all the cop shows on TV, most people know better than to hide a murder weapon in their room. Naturally, we'll check into Mr. Stoddard's background and finances to look for a motive. But if no one had a reason to kill him, then we have to consider the possibility that Mr. Langdon was the target."

I looked at him, noting that he wasn't being quite so "Aw, shucks" as before. "So then you'll ask a whole new set of questions tomorrow? Go over all the statements one by one trying to figure out who wanted to kill one man—and killed another by mistake?"

"We have to get at the truth," he said doggedly.

I suddenly felt very tired. "There are a lot of truths

in this house, Captain. And probably quite a few lies. But I can't believe there's a murderer.''

''You just don't want to believe it, and we both know it.'' Those spaniel-brown eyes were sharp and hard then, and his voice held the same kind of edge I'd heard in Trey's voice a few too many times—a cop's edge.

I thought of Peter's strange mood. The way Innis had angered nearly everyone so many hours ago at lunch. Mother's pale face. Adam's cold eyes. Vanessa's possible entanglement with Innis. Grace's pinched features. I remembered Maddy slapping Innis, and wondered if Cain had seen. (He'd made the drinks. Damn. *Damn.*) I remembered Cain's unnaturally fixed expression at lunch—everybody's expression at lunch. And then I thought of all the closed faces I'd seen in the parlor across the hall.

Long minutes passed while the cops in the room watched me.

No, I didn't want to believe it.

I'd never wanted to run so badly in my life.

In a voice that shook slightly despite my efforts, I said, ''If you'll tell me who to give my statement to, Captain, I'd like to do that. And then I think I'll go for a walk—if that's all right with you, of course.''

Winslow glanced at Trey, then motioned for the officer with the clipboard and told him to get my statement in one of the other rooms. I followed him out without looking at either Winslow or Trey again.

ALL RIGHT, I know what you're thinking. Something like: Boy, she's a real bitch, isn't she?

Well, maybe so. The only person I could justifiably blame for the situation was the murderer—if there was one—and I didn't want to know who that was (which meant I couldn't scream at him or her for doing this to me). At the same time, I didn't like the idea of *not* knowing who it was. I mean, if you're reasonably sure one of your relatives killed another one, but you don't know which one it was, then the entire family is apt to be a little uptight about it.

Like Jason, I sometimes get flippant when I'm worried and anxious. Keep it in mind.

The point was, as hard as I'd been trying to deny it, I knew Trey was right. Lawrence had been murdered, probably when someone had been aiming at Innis. And he had to have gotten the poison while we were all together in the room; arsenic, in sufficient doses, is not a slow-acting poison, so not even Lawrence could have been walking around with the stuff inside him for long before he died.

Besides, Winslow had said there was sediment in the glass—which meant that he'd certainly been poisoned then and there. And *that* meant everyone in the house except the family would be ruled out as suspects. None of the staff had even been in the room, and no convenient stranger had been present during the time we'd been gathered there.

So. Like it or not, there would be a murder investigation. Like it or not, there wasn't much doubt the question would ultimately be not "Who killed Lawrence?" but "Who wanted to kill Innis?"

And there were a host of suspects.

I thought the police would probably find the rat poison (or whatever) stored somewhere around, placed conveniently where anyone could get at it.

Means.

We'd all been in the room, moving around restlessly, and a convincing argument could be made for the idea that any of us *could* have wandered by and slipped a lethal dose into Lawrence's glass without being seen by the others (whether or not we believed it was Innis's glass we were doctoring).

Opportunity.

That left motive. The police really didn't have to prove motive in most cases. In this case, however, I thought it was literally the only way to narrow the field of suspects. Since we'd all had means and opportunity, and since no dandy bit of circumstantial evidence had been found, motive was the only thing left for Winslow to work with.

I didn't doubt that nearly all of us had, at one time or another, felt the impulse to murder Innis. But one of us had felt more than an impulse. The police—meaning Trey and Winslow—were going to have to try and find out who that was. They would have to dig and probe and ask very difficult questions. They would, undoubtedly, uncover a few irrelevant secrets along the way. Irrelevant to the investigation, that is.

Not irrelevant to the family.

I'd watched another family go through pure hell during a murder investigation when their secrets were exposed. And it had left me sickened and shaken because I had been the one to do that to them.

I couldn't be the one now. Please, God, I couldn't. Even though Winslow had asked for my help. Even though I had the numb feeling that Trey would ask me point-blank—again, for the second time since I'd met him—to look for a murderer because I had the knack of finding things. He was a cop, so he'd ask. No matter what it cost him. No matter what it cost us.

Murder was wrong, he'd say. And I agreed with that. Usually.

But. I'd already seen the sense of betrayal some of my relatives felt because I'd neglected to warn them Trey was a police officer. How would they feel toward me if they saw me step over the line and take an active part in the investigation of my own family? How would they feel if I were the one to dig and probe and question?

This was *my* family, goddamn it! I didn't like all of them, but I loved some of them, and hated only one. Par for the course, I suppose, where families were concerned. In any case, I owed them a certain amount of loyalty, didn't I?

Didn't I?

I GAVE THE officer—whose name was Jordan—my statement, keeping it simple and succinct. I didn't offer thoughts, suppositions, or speculations, merely detailed my movements from just after breakfast until Lawrence died. (Being a licensed private investigator does teach you a few things.) My statement would be typed and returned the following day for my signature, I was told. And if I thought of anything else, any detail which presently eluded me, I should let them know.

I knew the drill.

With that over, I left the house. Fled, really. It wasn't raining now, but it was dark outside, still cloudy with no moon showing, and there was quite a bit of wind. The darkness didn't bother me; I knew the grounds the way most people know their backyards.

I took off my shoes (we dressed for dinner, remember?) and carried them, not giving a particular damn that I was ruining my hose. I just walked. Through the garden and out across a field that wasn't pastured but was used for cutting hay. Since it was early spring, the grass was just beginning to come up, and the ground was soggy from the rain.

I walked for a long time.

Like most wandering souls, I moved in a circle, ending up back at the house. Back where I'd started. I wasn't quite ready to go in yet, so I sat in one of the lounges on the dark veranda, and just listened to the crickets. My eyes had adjusted by then, so I could see fairly well, but I wasn't looking at anything in particular.

It occurred to me to wonder if the others had eaten dinner. Some of them had, probably. If I knew Alexander, those who hadn't eaten would find something waiting for them in their rooms, sandwiches or soup in an insulated dish. Something. In times of crisis even more than normality, Alexander was a godsend, unobtrusive and efficient as he went about the task of making everyone's life easier.

Trey would know that Alexander, if he wished, could be a font of information about the family. But that "if" was a big one. I wasn't sure Alexander would talk to Trey, or at least open up to him. I knew he would to me.

Damn. Damn, damn, *damn.*

"Wauur?"

My cat jumped onto the lounge and sat down beside my legs, his china-blue eyes catching some stray gleam of light and glowing the way cats' eyes do. I reached out to scratch under his chin, and realized my hands were cold only when I felt how warm Choo was.

"Hello, cat," I murmured. "Where've you been?"

The reply was a sort of squeaky rumble, since Choo had his chin raised in blissful enjoyment. I felt a few sticky bits of beggar lice near his collar, and pulled the little seeds—I think they're seeds, anyway—out of his thick fur. That was the answer to my question: he'd been roaming out in the fields. (Choo's a neutered tom, but cats love to explore even when they're not driven by their hormones.) I automatically checked him over for other unpleasant examples of flora or fauna he might have picked up, and found nothing except a few more bits of beggar lice.

After that, I just sat there petting him and listening to him purr.

There's something about stroking a cat which is very soothing. As I understand it, some care facilities for abused kids and mentally disturbed people have discovered that cats and dogs actually benefit patients. Even doctors admit that you can lower your blood pressure by snuggling up with the family dog or taking a cat onto your lap.

It worked for me that night. There was no magical answer to all my problems, of course, but—eventually—I thought that I could at least face them.

I was scared, though, for a number of reasons. First, and most importantly, I had to face the knowledge that if I didn't find some way to deal with my ambivalence about Trey being a cop, I wouldn't get a third chance. Not because he would get fed up with me, but because I couldn't handle the pain and stress of another murder investigation—inside my own family this time—if Trey and I were on opposite sides.

I didn't think he could, either.

Does that sound selfish? I mean, with a murder having occurred in the house behind me, you might think I was being a little self-centered in brooding over my love life. But the point was, I couldn't nerve myself up to face my relatives unless and until Trey and I found a very solid bit of common ground from which to deal with the situation without tearing each other to pieces. We had to reach some agreement, or else I'd be useless to him *and* to my family.

I hadn't exactly shown my best colors since the murder, you must admit. And it would only get worse, I knew, unless I could get all this sorted out.

But on the very thorny point of murder, Trey and I were about as different as two people could be, and that was the major cause of the current tension between us.

He asked difficult questions and did an impossibly painful job because he believed it was necessary. Because the tragic waste of lives was something a man of conscience simply couldn't let pass unchallenged. So he had chosen to fight, accepting the laws his society laid down and working to enforce them.

Unlike me and so many others, Trey didn't have the luxury of asking himself murky philosophical questions. He would have gone mad long ago if he had blindly followed the moral contortions diverse segments of society endlessly debated, questioning the laws because others did. Instead, and rightly so, he left that to courts and judges and voters. As long as the laws were judged fit, he was bound to uphold them.

Black and white. Good and bad. Right and wrong.

For Trey, there couldn't be any gray areas, any murky uncertainties. Because if there were, everything his life stood for would be called into question. Everything *he* stood for would be meaningless.

I knew that. I even understood it. With me, however, there always seemed to be a "but . . ." or a "what if . . ."

Murder is wrong, yes—but what if it's justified? Is it murder then? What if there are reasons to pardon a seemingly unpardonable act? What if the victim is a hundred times worse than his killer?

Is it still murder?

Who am I to make those distinctions?

That was, as they say, the rub. Trey had decided where he stood, and he took responsibility for his beliefs and his actions. Knowing there were no absolute truths in life, he had chosen the black and white lines of law, and depended on evidence, instinct, and knowledge to guide him to truth.

Me, I was still debating all the damned questions. Not only was I all too aware of gray areas everywhere, but I was afraid to trust myself, afraid to take a stand—because I might be wrong. Because I didn't want to be the prosecutor, judge, jury, or hangman, and take responsibility for adversely affecting someone's fate.

Because I might be wrong.

You may wonder if I came to some resolution out there in the dark with my cat. If you know me (and by now you probably do), I'm sure you've guessed that I didn't. Come to a resolution, I mean. The best that can be said of all that agonizing is that I sort of clarified the problem. The truth was, I knew I couldn't figure it out alone.

It wasn't just my problem.

It was a case of *me*, yes—but it was even more a case of *us*. If I hadn't been in love with a cop, I probably would have gone on quite contentedly for years—maybe for always—debating the issues and bolting at the first twinge of pain. But being in love does a funny thing. All of a sudden, it isn't just you. It can't be. Like suddenly discovering your shadow as a child, being fascinated and a bit unnerved by the realization that it's attached to you always, you have to learn how to be comfortable with something that's separate—yet part of you.

After a while, I got up from the lounge and went into the house through the solarium. Choo didn't come with me, which made me wonder if he sensed death in the house. Animals do, you know. Anyway, I went in alone, and locked the French doors behind me. I supposed Alexander had left them open for me, or had looked out at some point and seen me on the veranda.

It was late—nearly midnight, according to my cat watch. The house was quiet, with the usual lamps left on. As I passed the library, I heard voices, and paused long enough to identify Trey, Mother, Adam, and Jason. I didn't linger to hear what they were discussing, but went on silently. I still wasn't ready to face anyone.

The living room doors were closed; I was willing to bet they were locked, and that Trey had the key. Not that I expected anyone to object; that room wouldn't be very popular for a long time to come.

Carrying my shoes, I climbed the stairs to the third floor, and went into our suite. I was very tired, physically as well as emotionally, so it was easy to keep my mind blank while I showered and put on a long nightgown. My habit is to sleep naked, and Trey had seen me in a nightgown only a couple of times in the very beginning. I wondered if he'd take note of my choice tonight. Probably. A cop's eye for detail.

The bed was turned down and ready, but I avoided it. I also avoided the table set up near one of the windows, where covered dishes and an insulated pitcher promised a substitute for the missed dinner. Instead, feeling a little chilled, I lit the gas fire in the fireplace and curled up in the scarlet gent's chair. Legs drawn up and feet tucked underneath me, I stared at the dancing flames.

It must have been nearly an hour later when Trey came in. He didn't say anything at first, just slowly crossed the room to stand by the hearth. Finally, in a guarded tone I didn't much like, he asked, "Would you rather I slept in another room?"

"No." I could feel myself frowning as I answered him. I wanted to say more than that, to say of course not or tell him I loved him or say anything to break the awful tension in the room. But I couldn't. I hated confrontations, but that one had to be endured, and I was scared to death that something desperately important would be in splinters when it was over.

After a moment, Trey moved away. I was still staring at the fire and heard him stirring around behind me. When he returned to the hearth, he'd shed his coat and tie, and looked less formal. But when I glanced at his face, it was the same mask he'd worn since Lawrence's death.

And again in that guarded tone, he said, "Nick will be back in the morning with the statements. He wants to go over each person's individually, just as you thought, before they sign them. He'll try to find a motive anyone might have had to kill Lawrence, but he's pretty well convinced Innis was the target, so he'll be looking for those motives too. I agreed to be present in the room when he goes over the statements—and he wants you to be there as well."

After all my agonizing, I had hoped I'd be able to view the prospect of helping the police (if I did) with at least a suggestion of detachment. It was a lost hope. I thought of sitting in a closed room while my family was brought in one by one to answer difficult questions, my presence there a sign to them that some lies would be recognized and pointed out, that my knowledge of them would be used against them, and a sick feeling churned in my stomach.

I didn't think I could do it.

I managed, somehow, to hold my voice steady and keep my tone objective. "I don't know why he wants me there," I lied. "I won't be any help to him."

Trey drew a short breath, and this time the strain showed. "You know why. Nick's an outsider. So am I, especially now. Some of them are bound to lie, or conceal things they believe aren't important, and that will make all this drag on even longer. That's where we need your help. You know your family, all the tensions and undercurrents. You can keep us from chasing down every blind alley."

My nice, neutral voice splintered. "Jesus, Trey, don't do this to me."

Trey has excellent command over his own features. In other words, he has a marvelous poker face when needed. During the Townsend investigation, I had rarely seen any emotion reflected in his face, though his voice had often told me much more than any expression could have.

That was then.

Now, he didn't try to hide anything. The mask was gone. I could see, very clearly, what he was feeling. Anger, pain, a certain amount of bitterness. And the intense reluctance of a cop asking for something the man in him knew was going to inflict anguish.

"Goddamn it, Montana, do you think I *like* this? It's the second time you could accuse me of using you. Maybe I had the excuse of not knowing you very well the first time. Maybe. But I know you now. I know you have a horror of influencing someone else's fate. I know the last thing on earth you want to be is a spy inside your own family. I know you'd like to run away from this. I know what I'm asking."

"Then don't," I said shakily.

"I have to. That was my answer before, wasn't it? I have to, because I'm a cop. I have to, because I believe you can help me find the truth."

"Not me. Somebody else." My throat was hurting. "I know I'm a coward, but I just—don't ask me to help condemn one of my own family!"

"Judges and juries condemn," Trey said. "All the rest of us do is try to find the truth. Montana . . . I don't know how to make it easier for you. I don't even know if I should. All I can tell you is what I believe. Murder is never an acceptable solution to a problem. Never."

"But—"

"No. No buts." He moved suddenly, taking a step to sit down on the stool in front of my chair. His voice was calm with certainty, and his luminous eyes had never looked so clear. "You can feel sorry for the killer as well as the victim. You can mourn the stupid, senseless waste of two lives—or three or four. You can condemn the environment or poverty, or even pity some poor bastard who was born without a conscience. But no one can be allowed to believe they won't pay a price for taking another human life. Montana . . . if we make killing easy, then no life counts for anything."

Struggling to voice my confused thoughts and feelings, I said, "But there are so many gray areas. Insanity, self-defense, abuse, euthanasia, abortion. How can we make a blanket statement to answer so many questions?"

"We can't. That's why there are degrees of murder and manslaughter, why a self-defense plea can be accepted if it's proven, and why laws are changed when they're determined to be unjust. That's why this society needs people like you who question and debate and challenge—to make sure the laws are as fair as we can humanly make them.

"But it needs people like me, too. People who enforce the laws because they *are* the laws. The rules we live by. You can't go on blaming me for believing in the job I have to do, any more than I can blame you for your doubts and questions."

He hesitated, then said steadily, "We can't let a difference in beliefs come between us again and again until it tears us apart. I don't want that, and I don't think you do."

SIX

FINALLY, one of us had said it. For some reason, I was glad it had been him.

I shook my head, then asked, "So how do we live with it?"

"All we can do is try to understand each other. Find a compromise if we can. Talk about it when it's a problem."

"Like now?" I managed a very faint laugh.

Trey smiled slightly. "Like now. I don't expect you to forget I'm a cop, but . . . Don't ever look at me as an enemy again, Montana. Please."

That hit a nerve, but this time I didn't shy away. He was right. I'd felt unreasonably betrayed since Lawrence had died, blaming Trey for a situation he hadn't created, and that's what had brought us to this confrontation. Because I couldn't run from or otherwise escape what was happening to my family, I had struck out at him.

"I'm sorry," I said.

He shook his head slightly. "We started off badly, you and I, and we've never really gotten back on track. If the Townsend mess had been a clear-cut case of an

evil killer and an innocent victim, I think things would
be different between us. But it wasn't. Everyone was in
pain—the killer most of all. And I made you face that
pain. The only way you could handle it then was to
blame me. Once you did that, all your questions and
doubts about how our society handles murder got tangled up with me being a cop and using that . . . authority to force you into a situation you hated. That
meant there was a part of me—of who I am—that you
couldn't trust."

I was glad he had realized that; it made it easier for
me to face it. "Yeah, I—I've been thinking about that.
I haven't been very fair to you, have I?"

He smiled crookedly. "Hey, our timing was lousy;
we both have to accept part of the blame for that. But
it *is* something we have to work out. Given the fact that
you aren't a usual type of P.I., the odds are against
both of us being involved in murder investigations. Still,
it happened once. And now it's happened again. You
and I are going to have to find a way of handling it, or
neither one of us is going to be any good—to each other
or to anyone else."

"Any suggestions?" I asked, having pounded my
head against the proverbial wall on that point.

Trey hesitated, then said, "Just one."

"Which is?"

"Turn the problem around, look at it from a different
direction. I doubt we'll ever agree on all the gray areas
you see between black and white. True?"

It was my turn to hesitate, but I finally nodded. If
you've been paying attention, you know the tortuous
path that had led me to that realization.

Trey spoke slowly. "All right, then. I say we don't
have to. All we have to agree is that our part—yours

and mine—in any situation like this one is to find the truth. Me because it's my job, and you because you have the ability to see things others miss. It isn't my or your responsibility to do anything else. There are attorneys, judges, and juries whose job it is to sort through all the legal and moral issues, and a system of law we *have* to accept, even with all its problems, because there's none better in the world.''

I was silent for a minute, then said wryly, ''In other words, I have to stop being afraid of condemning someone because I won't be the one doing it?''

He lifted an eyebrow at me, just as wry. ''Montana, your knack of cutting through all the bullshit is one of the things I love about you.''

I couldn't help but smile. ''Look, intellectually I know you're right. Emotionally I can't help feeling responsible when I do anything that affects someone's life. I don't know why that's my own personal nemesis, but it is.''

''I know. But if you can just bring yourself to believe that sometimes—especially in the case of murder—the most potentially tragic and painful choice is to do nothing when you *can* affect the outcome, then maybe you can put that sense of responsibility into perspective.''

This time, I frowned. ''What do you mean?''

''Well, take this case—''

''Do we have to?'' I interrupted.

''We have to talk about it sooner or later. Like it or not, it isn't going away.''

Sometimes I hate rational people. ''All right,'' I said unwillingly. ''This case, then.'' Poor Lawrence; now he'd been reduced to a ''case.''

Trey might have guessed what I was thinking, because he looked wry again, but he didn't comment on that. Instead, he said, "A man's dead. A man who, as far as we know, was utterly inoffensive and harmless. And someone in this house murdered him. In a situation like this, every innocent person involved is going to suffer all the more if we don't find the truth."

"Maybe, but—"

"You know it's true. I'm willing to bet you've been looking at most of your relatives in a different way since Lawrence's death. Wondering. Asking yourself which one of them is capable of murder. Haven't you?"

Reluctantly, I nodded.

"All right. Now suppose, just for the sake of argument, that you are the only one who could find the truth. If you do nothing, no one will ever know who killed Lawrence."

"That isn't a valid argument," I protested. "There's no way I could be the only one."

Ruthlessly, Trey said, "But that's the whole point. You *are* the only one, *in your mind,* who's responsible if you in any way help uncover evidence against a murderer. That's the way you feel. So I'm putting you in the actual situation. No one else has a clue. The police are helpless, and the case is unsolved. If you don't act, it never will be solved."

Just the idea made me uncomfortable, but I nodded unwillingly. "Okay. And so?"

"Well, do you act or don't you? If you act, one of your relatives will be arrested for murder. If you don't act, no one will ever know who did it."

For the sake of argument, hell. Even though I couldn't believe that only I could solve a murder, Trey was making his point in Technicolor.

I was chewing on my thumbnail, and didn't even try to make myself stop. He was being so goddamned reasonable and rational and—and I knew he was right. About the truth, at least. The family was being shaken, as precarious as a house made of playing cards, and it would collapse just as easily in the erratic winds of suspicion and mistrust.

But it didn't make it easier, knowing that.

"What if we never find the truth? Could you live with that?" he asked quietly. "Never knowing for sure who the killer is? Looking at your relatives in a way you never have before, because you know one of them is capable of murder—and you don't know which one. How can you *not* act, when the choice of doing nothing will tear your family apart?"

He shook his head slightly, still gazing at me very steadily. "And what if that murderer did kill the wrong man? What if it isn't over?"

I laced my fingers together tightly in my lap, and with all the calm I could muster, asked, "What if the killer is someone I care about?" That was my greatest fear. But Trey's answer made me face an equally horrible possibility.

"What if the next victim turns out to be someone you care about? If Lawrence was a mistake—someone else could be another mistake."

"He wouldn't dare, not now," I objected quickly.

"That depends on his motives, doesn't it? If he's desperate enough, and if Lawrence was a mistake, then he'll try again. And I'm told that after the first kill, it gets easier."

Both of us were using the masculine pronoun for convenience, though if you counted the people in the house—including us and excluding the servants—we were equally divided by sex; the killer could easily be a woman.

''Montana, no matter how painful it is, sorting out the guilty from the innocent is always the best thing to do. Because if it isn't done, everyone suffers for it, *especially* the innocent. And because, if someone gets away with murder, we've helped to make life cheap.''

I'd be lying if I said that Trey's certainty had rubbed off on me, but he had made his case. In the abstract, his points were valid; in the specific, I wouldn't be able to live with myself if I stood by and did nothing while a murder and its aftereffects destroyed my family.

Finding the truth could cause the same thing, if the truth was bad enough—but never finding it was a gilt-edged guarantee that it *would* happen. And even though I didn't have the same faith Trey showed in my so-called ability to see things other people missed, if I could help find the truth, I had to.

Sighing, I said, ''All right. I'll try to remember that I'm not a judge or a jury, and keep all the painful issues in perspective. I don't know if I can, but I'll try. And . . . I'll try to help you and your friend—who is not by any stretch of the imagination the hick he pretends to be—find out what happened in this house and why.''

If Trey was feeling as emotionally exhausted as I was just then, he was probably grateful to pick up on the lighter part of my agreement. In any case, he did.

''Nick didn't fool you, huh?''

''No. Oh, he's good, I'll give him that. Some of the others will certainly buy his act.''

''I told him you wouldn't. But I believe he wanted to see for himself.'' Trey reached over and took my hands in his, smiling a little.

Until then, we hadn't touched at all, and I think both of us had been conscious of it. Now, as always, I was very much aware of the contact. His hands had affected me peculiarly from the first time I'd seen them—so raw-boned, ugly, and brutally powerful when the rest of him was so elegant. It was difficult for me to think clearly when he touched me, as I believe I've mentioned.

A little vaguely, I said, "Alexander had food sent up for us. Or have you eaten?"

"No. I was a bit—upset after Nick and his men left, so I spent some time talking to Jason, your mother, and Adam. Elizabeth wants you and me to stay here in the house until all this is resolved."

"Is that a good idea?"

"I don't know. We'll wait and see what happens to-morrow."

Since I didn't want to think about tomorrow until I had to, I let that subject slide away into limbo. I couldn't help wondering, though, at Mother's willingness to have Trey and me remain in the house when the majority of the others would undoubtedly want us out of there. Did she believe, as Trey did, that the truth had to come out no matter what?

As Trey rose and pulled me to my feet, I couldn't help asking, "Are we going to make it through this?"

"We're sure as hell going to try," he replied.

I BELIEVE I told Trey I loved him that night mostly because I was so damned tired. I was sort of without defenses, if you know what I mean. Otherwise, I probably would have kept the knowledge to myself as long as possible. (It scared me, remember?)

In any case, neither of us was hungry just then, and despite weariness we weren't ready for sleep. Trey took a shower, and somehow or other I ended up in there with him—an interlude which led quite naturally to lovemaking. (You wouldn't think either of us could find the energy, but that wasn't a problem.) And at some point, charged with passion and a peculiarly helpless feeling of anger, I told him.

I probably would have panicked if he'd answered the declaration with silence, but he was reassuringly prompt (and even a little relieved, I think) in saying he loved me.

Aren't relationships strange? There we were, two people with a rocky road behind us and a treacherous stretch ahead, surrounded by a houseful of uneasy people (one of whom had apparently killed today), physically weary and emotionally vulnerable, and we took the insane risk of picking that time—of all times—to admit how we felt about each other. Crazy, both of us.

Then again, maybe that was the only time we—or I, at least—could have done it.

Anyway, I have to say that the remainder of that night was the first time Trey and I had been completely in sync. There didn't seem to be any awkward places or pauses. I suppose we shut out the rest of the world, which is, I believe, hardly an original practice between lovers. Nice, though. It was around three A.M. when we crawled out of bed to polish off Alexander's snack, and then we went back to bed and talked for another couple of hours. All right, we didn't *just* talk, but we talked, too.

I don't remember how we got onto the subject of my parents, not clearly. I suppose it was natural, though. When all the walls come tumbling down, the gremlins crouching in the dark corners are suddenly visible. I couldn't hide them anymore—or hide from them. But, for the first time, I didn't feel blind panic when Trey made a very neutral observation.

"You must have been very young when you lost your father."

I sat up in our absurd bed and wrapped my arms around my upraised knees, staring across the shadowy room at the gas fire turned down low in the fireplace. I wished it were completely dark in the room. Even when you're willing, some things are easier in the dark.

"Montana?" He sat up beside me, and I felt one of his hands lightly stroke my bare back. It was a soothing touch, as if he sensed a need to comfort me.

Without looking at him, I said very steadily, "I was ten. There was no warning, not that I saw. Everything seemed fine. He'd taken Jase and me to the circus that afternoon." Parenthetically, I added, "You know, I haven't been to see a circus since, even though I thought it was the best place in the whole world to be."

I felt something warm touch my shoulder, and realized vaguely that he had kissed me there. But I still didn't look at him. Against my will, I was being dragged back through time, more than twenty years into the past, and feeling things I'd promised myself I would never feel again.

"We came home and had supper," I went on in that same unnaturally normal voice. "And there was nothing different, no warning. He didn't even say good-bye. He just . . . left the house that night, while we were getting ready for bed. He was out of cigarettes, he told Mother, and the store would close at eleven. He never came back."

Trey's hand stilled but continued to touch me. "Did anything happen to him?"

I shook my head. "No, nothing happened to him. He wasn't in a wreck. Nobody robbed the store where he bought cigarettes. Nobody kidnapped him. Nothing

. . . kept him from coming back home. He just didn't.
I found out much later that he had cleaned out the bank
accounts and borrowed cash up to the limit on all his
charge accounts the day he left. So it was planned. He
called Mother late the next afternoon, before the police
would accept a report of a missing person because he
hadn't been gone long enough. I don't know what he
said to her, but it was the only time in my life I've seen
her cry.''

"I'm sorry," Trey said softly.

I had never talked about my father to anyone before,
except Jase—and we hadn't talked about him in years.
Now, with Trey, once I'd started, I couldn't seem to
stop. My voice might have been coming from someone
else for all the control I had over the words.

"For a long time, I wouldn't believe he'd just walked
away. I couldn't believe that. I made up all kinds of
stories about why he couldn't come back to us. At one
point, I decided he'd been killed. Even that didn't hurt
as much as accepting the fact that he'd abandoned us.
I . . . couldn't understand how a father could walk away
from his own flesh and blood, and never come back.
As if he just . . . stopped caring. For years after, on
birthdays and at Christmas, I hoped for something. Even
a card. But there was never any word at all.''

"Is he still alive?"

"I don't know. After twenty-one years, I rarely ask
myself that question anymore. In a way, I don't want
to know. Does that make sense?"

"I think so." Trey was silent for a few moments,
then said, "What about your mother?"

I rested my chin on my upraised knees, staring so
hard at the fire in the fireplace that it had gone all blurry.
"What about her?"

"Was she a good mother before your father left?"

The question caught me off-guard, because it wasn't what I'd expected. "I . . . suppose." There was something about Trey's silence that was like being stared at intently—or maybe he was; I wasn't looking at him. Anyway, I couldn't offer just a two-word answer to his question.

"Yes, she was. She was always wrapped up in Daddy, but—" I broke off abruptly, surprised and a little unnerved by that childlike term for my father.

Trey wouldn't let me stop, for whatever reason. "But?"

I cleared my throat. "But—she always had time for Jase and me. She read to us. Started Jase with finger-paints, then watercolors. I was a jigsaw-puzzle fiend; she spent hours helping me put them together."

"And after your father left? What then?"

That was the question I'd expected earlier, and I could feel tension building inside me. Even when you're willing, some gremlins have to be dragged, kicking and screaming, from their dark corners. I wasn't at all sure I was willing to do that.

Gremlins? Hell, that one was more like a dragon.

"Montana?"

I almost heard the voice across twenty years, that high, childish voice that had been mine, screaming an accusation out of confusion and anguish. God, I *did* hear the voice.

Some thoughts and feelings, some nasty little voices inside us, should stay locked away forever. But sometimes they break loose. And nobody can take back a thought once it's put into words. Especially an ugly, painful thought. Maybe an apology would help at least a little, but with every passing year it becomes harder to utter those simple words.

Until it becomes impossible.

I didn't realize I was rubbing my chin methodically back and forth over my knees—hard—until Trey's hand slid up my spine and gently touched the rigid nape of my neck.

I lifted my chin and cleared my throat again, still gazing across the room at the blurry glow of the fire. "She was different. We all were." I hesitated, then said, "Trey—can we go into all this later?"

Quietly, he said, "You have to face your ghosts sometime."

"I call 'em gremlins." I half laughed, then turned my head finally to look at his shadowy face, the gleam of his eyes. "And . . . I know they have to be dragged out into the light. But not all of them at once, okay? We have time, don't we?"

"You're a stubborn woman, Montana."

"Yeah. But if that's the worst thing you can say about me, I'm luckier than most."

He must have realized I'd gone as far as I could that night, because he didn't push. And since the haunting voice in my head had faded mercifully into silence, nothing tempered my usual response when he kissed me. In fact, I might have been even more passionate than usual.

Maybe confession is good for more than just the soul.

IT HAD TO be nearly dawn before we fell asleep. Normally, as I've mentioned, waking up is a problem for me, especially without a solid eight or ten hours behind me, but Trey didn't have any trouble waking me up around nine. And I felt surprisingly rested, all things considered.

I also felt less tortured about the situation in the house. Not comfortable with my role, mind you, but since I did agree the truth had to be found for everyone's sake, and since it *was* my family, I could hardly go on yelling that somebody else had to do it.

So I'd actually made two commitments in the dark watches of the previous night. The one to Trey and to our relationship (it was the first time since my college sweetheart that I'd ever told a man I loved him), and the one to the investigation into Lawrence's death.

Of the two, I didn't know which one would turn out to be more painful.

Nick Winslow was scheduled to return to the house in the early afternoon, Trey had told me, and between that looming and just generally facing the wariness and/or hostility of some of my relatives, I wasn't particularly looking forward to the day ahead of us. But since I wasn't so jumbled up as I had been the day before, I have to admit that morning brought the purely intellectual puzzle of Lawrence's death to the forefront of my mind.

"Was he poisoned while we were all in the room with him, or could it have happened earlier?" I asked Trey as we were going downstairs for breakfast. "Are you reasonably sure the sediment in his glass was poison?"

In the same detached tone I had used, Trey replied, "Until we get the autopsy and lab results, we won't know for certain. But I'm as sure as I've ever been about anything that he was poisoned in that room right under our noses. The stuff was slipped into his glass."

"And meant for Innis?"

"The first rule of detecting—as you well know—is never assume. So we'll keep our eyes and ears open for a motive someone might have had to kill Lawrence. As far as I could tell, though, there was nothing but shocked surprise in that room, and I'd swear it was genuine." Trey shrugged. "That someone could have been after Innis is more likely. And since the glasses could have been switched so easily, that gives more weight to the theory."

"Then Winslow will have to ask a completely different set of questions today, won't he?"

"He's planning to. Naturally, and according to procedure, Lawrence's background and finances will be checked out, just as Nick said. Since Lawrence made his home in Birmingham, the Alabama police will be asked to gather what information they can. He was a salesman, right?"

I nodded. "Computer software. He traveled all over the Southeast, and was on the road at least three weeks out of every month. Funny."

"What?"

"Well, I just find it hard to believe he could be a successful salesman. He almost never said anything around us, and trying to get him talking was nearly impossible. And you barely noticed he was around. He was so . . . invisible." I shrugged. "Still, he apparently made a good living as a salesman."

"Um. We'll have to find out how good a living . . . and get statements from some of his business associates."

"You don't expect to find a motive there, do you?"

"No, since his business had nothing to do with the family. Am I right about that?"

I'd felt a flicker of hope, but it died. "Yes, as far as

I know. Damn it, we're limited to the family no matter which way we go, aren't we?''

"I'm afraid so, Montana."

Broodingly, I said, "Practically everybody was mad at Innis by the time we met for drinks last night; as far as I could tell, nobody even noticed Lawrence. Something must have happened—in not much more than twenty-four hours—to make somebody mad enough to kill. I mean, we'd all put up with Innis for so many years that if anybody'd wanted him dead, they probably would have done it a long time ago. I doubt Lawrence said a dozen words to anybody from the time he got here; how could he have roused somebody to murder him?''

Trey sifted through my tangled statements and questions, and neatly condensed everything I was trying to say. "I think we both believe that Lawrence was a mistake, don't we?''

I looked up to meet his eyes, and sighed. "Yeah, I think we do. The other way just doesn't make sense, at least not with what we know of Lawrence. But we can't ignore the fact that Innis has been causing ripples for years. Granted, he's been worse this weekend than I can remember him being before, but what did he say or do to make somebody finally decide to put him out of our misery?''

"That," Trey said, "is what we have to find out."

We had reached the ground floor by then, and as we headed for the breakfast room, I said, "Doesn't it strike you as weird to be investigating the murder of a man who's still alive?''

"It's a bit different," Trey admitted dryly. "I'm a little curious to see how Innis reacts to the suggestion."

"He won't believe it." I was very sure of that. "In fact, he'll dismiss the very idea."

"Probably, given what I know of his personality. But will the rest of the family dismiss it?"

It was a rhetorical question, because both of us knew the answer.

In the breakfast room, we found Jason, Mother, Adam, and Vanessa, all of them going through the motions of eating. Adam seemed his usual calm self; Jason was alert—both troubled and, perhaps unwillingly, curious; Mother was pale and looked a bit tired; and Vanessa was sullen.

As we greeted them, I noted with interest that there were a couple of empty chairs between Jase and Vanessa (had she given up because of his lack of interest, or because of the murder?), but Adam spoke before I could think more about it.

"Trey, will Captain Winslow insist on getting a statement from Emily today?"

"With the other statements to go over, I doubt it," Trey replied. "Is she still sedated?"

Mother answered that, her voice strained. "The doctor gave her a shot last night, but left sedatives with me. I had to give her something about an hour ago, and Grace is sitting with her. I don't know what she's going to do now. She's always depended on Lawrence. For everything."

"What are *we* going to do?" Vanessa demanded tightly. "All those questions that cop asked me—personal questions! And looking through me with those awful eyes like he didn't believe a word I said. They searched my room! And what about when it gets out? When the newspapers and TV start running those awful reports?"

Calmly, Trey said, "As isolated as this house is, and since county police took the report, we may have a few days' grace before there's any publicity."

Vanessa stared at him with haughty dislike. "If you hadn't been here, we wouldn't have had a problem at all. *I* say he died of a heart attack or something. It's ridiculous to think anybody would have killed him. Why—he was *nothing.*"

Before anyone could respond to her strident remarks, Adam rose from his place, went around the table, and pulled Vanessa to her feet.

"Excuse us," he said.

I didn't like Vanessa, as I believe I've made clear, but I have to admit I felt a bit sorry for her as she was dragged sputtering from the room by her father.

Nobody said anything for a few minutes while Trey and I collected our breakfast from the sideboard, then Mother spoke ruefully as we sat down at the table.

"She's a difficult child, I'm afraid."

"Difficult?" Jason laughed shortly. "Mother, I like Adam a lot, I really do, but his daughter's a pain in the ass. She's been driving Alexander and the staff crazy, for one thing, expecting them all to fetch and carry for her. For another thing, she's a spiteful little cat. When I told her yesterday to leave me the hell alone, she picked up a big rock and smashed one of the windows on my car."

Obviously both shocked and upset, Mother said, "When was this? Why didn't you say something?"

Jason looked as if he wished he'd kept his mouth shut, and shrugged. "It's no big deal—I can get the window fixed. Besides, we've had other things to worry about."

Suddenly remembering what I'd heard on the veranda

yesterday after lunch, I said, "Did you two have a fight out in the garden, Jase?"

He blinked at me. "What? No, we didn't have a fight anywhere. I went out to my car just before we met for drinks last night, because I couldn't find the book I'd brought with me and thought it might be there. Vanessa—" He glanced at Mother, cleared his throat, and continued carefully. "Well, she followed me out there and made an offer I wouldn't care to repeat. I told her to get lost, and she smashed the window. Then she stormed back into the house, and I haven't said a word to her since."

I suppose I was frowning as I looked at my brother, because he was frowning back at me.

"Why did you ask," he demanded.

"No reason. I just wondered." I returned my attention to my plate, very aware that both Mother and Trey were looking at me—Mother a little puzzled and Trey thoughtfully. I didn't enlighten them, since I was trying to figure out just what it was that I'd heard out there.

A female voice crying out, "How could you?" That was what I'd heard. Vanessa? Shortly before that, I'd seen her and Innis cozily together in the solarium. If she'd had a fight with Innis and, a few hours later, heard Jason tell her to kiss off, it seemed Vanessa hadn't had a great day.

Spiteful, Jason had called her, and God knows he's pretty good at judging people. She had struck out at him, immediately and childishly, for rejecting her. Had Innis also rejected her (unlikely), or somehow insulted her (definitely possible)?

In one of those weird tricks of memory the human mind is capable of, I suddenly had a flash of something that had happened the night before. Vanessa prettily offering to get her (surprised) father a refill. Pausing beside Innis. Taking his glass as well.

At the time, I'd merely thought idly that she'd wanted to say something casual to Innis, but I wondered now if she hadn't seemed a little tense.

Hindsight? It's easy to look back and attribute emotions or motives that just weren't visible at the time. Was that what I was doing? Or had I really seen something in her posture or movements that had alerted me subconsciously?

Damn it, I didn't know.

Trey didn't say anything about my preoccupation until Mother excused herself a few minutes later. Since only the two of us and Jason were left in the room—and since, as I've said, Trey got along quite well with my brother and obviously trusted him—he asked me then.

"What's bothering you, Montana?"

I pushed my plate away and leaned back, fortifying myself with a sip of coffee. Then, slowly, I said, "Did Winslow or one of his cops dust Lawrence's glass for prints? Or was it just sent directly to the lab?"

"It was dusted here," Trey said. "Along with Innis's glass, since they were identical. Nick habitually carries a print kit, and he's good."

I was aware of Jason's interested attention but kept my gaze on Trey. "I see. Then, when I was asked to look at the room, you two had more than a suspicion that the glasses could have been switched. Because . . . there were at least two sets of prints on Lawrence's glass?"

Trey smiled very slightly. "That glass had been around. Complete prints from two people on both glasses, and partials on Lawrence's glass from, we believe, at least two more.''

''You didn't tell me that.''

''I didn't get the chance. Afterward, I mean.''

After a moment, I returned his smile. ''Fair enough.'' I hadn't, after all, given him much of a chance to confide in me. ''No wonder you've been so sure.''

''Sure about what?'' Jason asked. ''That it was murder?''

Trey looked at him. ''We're virtually positive it was murder. Certain poisons leave signs, and arsenic is one of them. He couldn't have taken it by accident, and I doubt very much that he was bent on committing suicide. What we're also fairly sure of is that Lawrence's death was a mistake. His glass and Innis's could have been accidentally switched.''

Something that Trey had said sort of rang a bell in my mind, but I wasn't sure what it was. All I could hope was that, if it was important, I'd remember later. The human mind tends to be a bit tricky about things like that, but from past experience I knew better than to worry over it. *That* would be an ironclad guarantee I'd never remember.

Jason thought about what he'd heard for a minute. ''You mean, somebody was trying to kill Innis? Oh, shit.''

My sentiments exactly.

''Is that all that was bothering you?'' Trey asked me.

''No. I just remembered something about last night, and that made me think about the glasses—and fingerprints. Early on, Vanessa got up to get Adam a refill. And she got one for Innis, too. If you find her prints on Lawrence's glass—and not on Innis's—it's another bit of proof they were switched.''

Trey nodded slowly, but he was watching me with his cop's eyes. ''What else?''

For the first time, that intent gaze didn't make me uncomfortable—maybe because I was finally succeeding in merging (in my mind) the man and the cop. In any case, I didn't hesitate to answer his question.

''I think Jason wasn't the only one Vanessa had her eye on. Innis, too.'' I explained about encountering her on the stairs the day before, what she'd said, and the fact that Innis had gone up shortly after, and shrugged. ''That's no proof, of course. But then, after lunch— Jase, remember when you were out there on the veranda with me? I told you Vanessa was in the solarium, and you bolted for the garden?''

''I remember. Why?''

''Well, I was about to add that Innis was with her, but you rushed off before I got the chance. Then, a few minutes later, Wanda blew your car's horn to summon you, and in the middle of all the noise I could swear I heard a woman yell 'How could you?' I didn't see anyone then, but if it was Vanessa . . .''

Jason pursed his lips thoughtfully. ''You mean, maybe they had a fight and she decided to get even?''

''Maybe. You rejected her, and she didn't hesitate to strike back. It isn't likely Innis did that; he wouldn't reject a willing blond if it was his only ticket into heaven. But we all know how ready he's been to insult all of us. If he insulted her, especially in some sexual way, she could have decided a little rat poison might be a fitting revenge.''

''Rat poison for a rat.'' Jason winced. ''Hell, she'd

think that way, too. You might be on to something, Lanie.''

Trey was nodding as well. ''Nick's planning to fingerprint everyone in the house—except you and me, since our prints are already on file.''

Speculatively, I said, ''I'm willing to bet the complete prints on the glass—on *both* glasses—belong to Innis and Lawrence. Anything else would just be too easy.''

Jason—not having served an apprenticeship as a private investigator—was a bit lost. ''What do you mean?''

Trey answered him. ''Identification by fingerprints works on a point system: a certain number of points are required for a positive I.D. With partial prints, we'll be lucky to get enough points to use for comparison.''

''In other words,'' Jason said, ''you might be fairly sure who the prints belong to, but it wouldn't stand up in court?''

''Right.''

I got up to get myself more coffee, thinking vaguely to myself that waking up with Trey did a better job of getting me in gear for the day than my usual reliance on caffeine. I'd been very clearheaded both yesterday morning and today, which was, to say the least, unusual for me.

Sometimes, being clearheaded can be a curse.

Rejoining the men at the table, I said broodingly, ''If Innis was the target, Vanessa can certainly be considered a suspect. But so can most of the rest of us. And whoever put the poison in didn't have to touch the glass. The way we were all moving around the room last night, virtually everyone was near the fireplace at one time or another, and it would have been simple to drop something into Lawrence's drink while it was sitting on the table. It could have been in a twist of paper or a corner cut from an envelope so it wouldn't have been obvious to anybody. If I'd done it, I sure as hell wouldn't have touched either of the glasses.''

"Did you notice Peter in the area?" Trey asked.

"No. In fact, I noticed he stayed as far away from his father as he could," I replied. Then, realizing, I added slowly, "But he was near the bar most of the time. When Vanessa brought the glasses for refills, I suppose he could have . . .''

Reluctantly, Jason pointed out the obvious. "He was acting strangely; we all noticed that and commented on it. Innis had been pushing him hard. And if the poison isn't found in the house—well, he did leave the grounds yesterday. He was the only one who did.''

"There's a good chance we have found the poison,'' Trey said. "Rat poison and a number of insecticides and other chemicals were found in the storage room out by the kitchen door. Samples have been sent to the lab.''

Great, I thought. That storage room was never locked, since there weren't small children about the place these days. So anybody could have slipped in there and mixed themselves a toxic potion suitable for a murder attempt.

Trey said slowly, "Peter was stunned when Lawrence died. Maybe because he knew it should have been Innis.''

We were all quiet for a few moments, then Jason spoke in a resolutely dispassionate voice.

"Okay, so Vanessa and Peter are possibles. Who else?''

He was looking at me, I could feel it. But I was staring at my coffee as hard as I could. I'd just had another of those damned memory flashes, and it made me acutely unhappy.

"Montana?" Trey's voice was quiet.

I half closed my eyes, then turned my head and met his.

"What else have you remembered?"

"Is my face so damned easy to read?" I demanded.

"Yes. What have you remembered?"

Truth, I reminded myself fiercely. We have to get at the truth. No matter what.

Still, I tried to make light of it. "Just something peculiar I saw, that's all. It might not mean anything."

"But it might be important." Trey was looking at me steadily, cop's eyes in a face I loved, and suddenly—without any warning at all—I felt the strangest sensation inside me. It was like something tearing open, painless but wet and warm.

I never want to feel that again, because it was the most deeply disturbing sensation I've ever felt in my life. But I'm glad I felt it that once. The only way I can define it is to say that the secret place inside me, the place all of us retreat to when we're hurting, and where we think we're alone—that place wasn't just mine anymore. Completely beyond my control, it had opened up to let Trey in.

I accepted my shadow. Accepted the cop I loved. And accepted my responsibility to find the truth.

Only seconds had passed, and when I spoke it was in the same dispassionate tone Jason had summoned earlier.

"Yesterday, before we came downstairs. We were getting ready; you were shaving, and I was in the sitting room of our suite fumbling with my earrings. I looked out the window and saw Maddy walking toward the house. Then I saw Innis. They stood there for maybe half a minute, talking. I couldn't see their faces clearly. Then Maddy slapped him."

It was Jason who spoke; Trey was still looking at me, and I had the feeling he felt or sensed what had happened to me. Or saw, I suppose, given my readable face. Jason was watching me closely as well, even though what I'd said obviously upset him, and that was what he talked about.

"Maddy? I've never seen Maddy lift a hand against anything, on two legs or four. She just doesn't have it in her, and you know it, Lanie. Besides that, Innis has always been more polite to her than anyone else."

"When Cain's around," I agreed, looking at my brother. "When all of us are around. But who knows what he might say or do if he found himself alone with her? She's exactly the type he's so hot for, Jase, and you know *that*. It doesn't make a damned bit of difference to him that she's his wife's sister-in-law."

"But with Cain in the house?" Jason said a bit helplessly. He loved both Maddy and Cain as much as I did, and I could see that the intellectual puzzle of a murder was rapidly losing its attraction for him.

I felt strangely calm. "He's been pushing the limit all weekend. Insulting or trying to pick fights with almost everybody. Besides, if he'd go so far as to make a play for Vanessa with his wife and her father under the same roof, what makes you think he wouldn't be willing to wave a red flag at Cain?"

Trey spoke slowly. "Cain has a temper?"

"A rare one. And only where Maddy's concerned," I answered, looking away from Jason's pale face to meet Trey's gaze. "But if he'd done it, you can forget poison. A gun or a knife, yeah, maybe. Even more likely, he would have beat Innis to a pulp. It would have been a hot-blooded killing, Trey, without any forethought—much less careful planning. There's no way it would have been a deliberate murder.''

In a jerky tone, Jason said, ''All this is pure speculation, anyway. We don't know that Cain had a reason, or that Maddy did. Maybe Innis said something offensive and she slapped him—period.''

''Maybe,'' I agreed. ''Maybe Peter didn't snap, and Vanessa didn't decide she needed revenge. Maybe Cain was pale at lunch yesterday because he felt queasy, and not because Innis had said something to make him furious. Maybe a lot of things. But somebody did it. That's not a maybe.''

I don't know what Jason would have said then, because I could see he was upset with me. I suppose I sounded a bit callous about the whole thing, at least to him. Trey was silent; he knew, more than Jason, the agonizing I'd gone through to earn that priceless detachment.

In any case, there was an interruption just then. Interruption. God.

Grace stood in the doorway of the room, her face very calm. She looked at us, focused on Trey and, in a mildly bemused tone, said, ''It's Innis. He's dead.''

SEVEN

GRACE AND INNIS'S suite was on the second floor, and about halfway down the eastside hallway. It was a very nice suite, decorated in French Provincial mostly but with a smattering of Great-Grandfather's peculiar touches.

Like the pretty figurine somebody had used to bash Innis's skull in.

It lay on the carpet about a foot from the chair he'd been sitting in, blood smeared over the jade representation of some Hindu god-figure. It made a dandy blunt instrument, since the head of the figure fit easily into most any size hand while the base was large and square, and the whole thing was heavy enough to be deadly without being especially unwieldy.

It had come from the small table beside the door, I knew, and had proven handy in that way as well since it was virtually the only practical object the killer could have found out of Innis's sight in the room before creeping up behind his chair and bashing him.

From the doorway, all I could see of Innis was one arm hanging limply from the side of the chair. It was a

high-backed chair with wings, so his head hadn't fallen
far enough sideways to be visible, and I was glad.

Trey was the only one who'd gone into the room,
other than Grace (and the killer, of course). He was
gone now to call Winslow, while Jason and I remained
at the door. Well, I was at the door; Jase was in the
hallway leaning against the wall about two feet away
from me, looking a little sick. I don't know how I
looked. The same, probably.

"Somebody must be damned desperate," he muttered. "I mean, hell, who in their right mind would kill
twice in less than twenty-four hours? And they all know
now that Trey's a cop, a *homicide* detective in the house,
with more cops due here in a few hours. It's insane."

I was looking at as much of the room as I could see
without going in, my mind fixed totally on trying to
spot something—anything—that was out of place. But I
wasn't very hopeful. It was clear to me that someone
had simply opened the door, stepped inside, picked up
the figurine, and struck Innis. The high back of the
chair made it unlikely that any blood had spattered on
the killer, and I was willing to bet whoever it was had
used gloves or a handkerchief. (After our TV educa-
tions, even kids know that much.)

Then merely drop the figurine on the floor, since it
belonged in the room and couldn't point to any one
person. After that, leave.

As murders go, it was relatively neat, simple, clean,
and quick. The entire thing couldn't have taken more
than a couple of minutes.

"You're very calm," Jason accused.

I slid my hands into the pockets of my jeans and
looked at him. "You think so?"

After a moment, Jason looked away. "Okay, maybe

not. But you're developing a hell of a poker face, Lanie.''

''No, it's not that. I'm just not quite so scared now because, unless I miss my guess, you, Mother, and Adam will be able to alibi each other.''

Jason stared at me. ''You didn't seriously suspect one of us of killing Lawrence?''

''Of course not. But the police might have. Jase, Lawrence was killed in a room where any of us could have done it, and every one of us, assuming Innis was the target, had reason—if only sheer dislike of Innis. Especially after lunch yesterday. Adam even threatened to throw him out of the house, and anybody could see you were mad as hell.''

''So were you,'' Jason commented.

''Yeah, well, the point is any of us could have done it. We all had the means and the opportunity. But this . . . this might turn out to be the killer's real mistake.''

''Why?''

''Because by killing Innis like this, he—or she—has eliminated several possible suspects. This time, all of us weren't gathered together in one room. From what he could tell from the body, Trey thinks it happened about two hours ago, certainly no longer than that, and his estimate is bound to be fairly accurate. It's eleven now. So, it probably happened, say, between nine and nine-thirty. Where were you then?''

Frowning, Jason replied, ''Downstairs. I went down about eight-thirty for coffee, and stayed in the breakfast room even though I wasn't very hungry. Adam came in around ten minutes later, saying that Mother and Grace were with Emily. Then Mother joined us maybe five minutes after that.''

''How about Vanessa?''

"She'd only been in the room about five minutes when you and Trey came down. That was—what?— about quarter to ten?"

"About. So you, Mother, and Adam can alibi each other from a little before nine o'clock until around ten. Trey and I can also alibi each other; even though the police tend to be skeptical when lovers alibi each other, Trey being a cop—and a stranger to the family—makes a difference. Grace was with Emily—but Emily was sedated, probably asleep. She was just now when I checked on her. Where's Wanda?"

"She came down right after me. Gulped a cup of coffee, then headed for the stables. Probably just wanted out of the house, poor kid."

"Then it's likely she has an alibi," I noted. "Not that anyone could seriously suspect Wanda, but I'll bet she was helping Reece with the horses when Innis met his maker." I thought about reasonable locations for my other relatives. "Kerry is probably still in bed—on this floor, though, damn it. What about Baxter? Have you seen him?"

Jason hesitated, then said, "He came down before you and Trey, sometime before ten. Drank some juice, then went out to run. He said Kerry was still asleep."

I wasn't particularly worried by that information; Baxter was not a man to do anything in haste or out of desperation, and this was, I thought, a hasty, desperate murder. As for Kerry . . . Well, let's just say I'd sooner believe Wanda had done it than Kerry. Not that the police would necessarily agree with me, but there were several far more likely suspects.

"Okay," I said steadily. "That leaves Cain and Maddy and Peter."

Grim, Jason said, "The three of them and Vanessa

seemed to be the strongest suspects for last night's debacle; now it's them again?''

''It looks that way. Unless, of course, they can produce believable alibis. Of the four of them, the only one we *know* without question had a strong motive is Peter. The rest is speculation, like you said.''

We fell silent for a while. Jason stared at the opposite wall, while I looked into the sitting room again. I couldn't see anything I thought might be important, but I looked anyway. You never know; something could have struck me.

There was Innis's breakfast tray on the coffee table near his chair; he had obviously eaten his last meal in peace. His newspaper (they were delivered to the house each morning, half a dozen copies) was on the floor, several sections stacked haphazardly as if they'd been dropped there when he finished with them, and one almost eerily tented section on the floor near his dangling hand. He'd probably been reading that one.

Judging by the position, the heavily crumpled look along one side of the section and the torn place on the other side, Innis had been holding that when the fatal blow was struck. His arm had probably jerked, his fingers tightening violently on the newspaper on one side and actually tearing a piece out of the other side. Blood had spattered, and when his arm dropped, the paper had fallen to the floor, landing on its top and bottom edges so that it tented in a slightly drunken fashion, with most of the spattered blood on the underside.

I couldn't see that any of that helped point an accusing finger at anyone.

''Did Grace eat breakfast?'' I asked idly.

''Mother had a tray sent up to her in Emily's room,''

Jason answered. ''I don't remember the time. Alexander will know, I expect.''

The house seemed very quiet. It seemed odd to me that this murder should have happened without most of the family even knowing about it, especially given Lawrence's very public death. It was ironic in a way. Lawrence, the invisible man of the family, had died in full view of all of us, while Innis the loudmouth had died neatly shut up in his room.

Few of the family even knew yet, or so I supposed. Grace was downstairs in one of the parlors with Mother and Adam; Jason had taken Grace in to them, explaining what had happened while Trey and I had come directly up here. We hadn't heard a peep from anyone else.

Even as the thought crossed my mind, Baxter came down the hall toward us—and toward his and Kerry's room at the end of the hall beyond—wearing sweats and looking flushed from his run. He stopped nearer to Jason than me, which meant he couldn't see into the room, and the automatic smile of morning greeting faded as he looked at us.

''What's happened?''

''Innis is dead,'' I replied, and wasn't surprised to see no real shock on his face. Surprise, yes, and I saw his gaze flit past us toward his and Kerry's suite, but I'd been right when I had told Trey that no one would be very much surprised if dear old Innis was found dead.

His voice was steady when he asked, ''How?''

Flippantly, Jason answered him. ''The traditional blunt instrument. In this case, a jade figurine briskly applied to the skull.''

Baxter's next question was purely a father's instinct. "Where's Wanda?"

"She's out with the horses," I told him. "She doesn't know. Neither does Kerry, I think."

Without another word, Baxter continued down the hall, and he didn't glance into Innis's room as he passed.

When we were alone again, Jason spoke in a methodical voice, the momentary flippancy gone. "Emily and Lawrence's suite is directly across the hall from Innis's; Vanessa's is a couple of doors down; and Kerry and Baxter's is at the end of the hall. Innis was served breakfast in his room as usual and so, apparently, was Grace—in Emily's room. So, either Alexander or, more likely, one or two of the maids have been on this floor at least twice this morning."

I nodded. "Innis was obviously served some time before he died, but he eats early, doesn't he?"

"Yeah, I think so."

"Okay. Then whoever served Grace is the best candidate for having noticed something. Maybe there was someone here in the hall, someone who didn't belong on this floor."

"Not Cain or Maddy," Jason muttered.

"It could have been either of them, Jase; they aren't accounted for so far. Could have been Peter. All three of them have rooms on the third floor with us."

Jason shifted his weight restlessly. "I don't like this very much, Lanie."

"No. Neither do I."

He looked at me, then said slowly, "I was mad at you downstairs before Grace came in. Sorry. You sounded pretty cold-blooded, I thought. But it's not that, is it?"

I didn't really know how to answer him, because I wasn't sure *what* it was. I was very worried, yet my mind was clear and peculiarly calm. Cautiously, I said, "I think last night wore me out, Jase. Between the bald truth of murder and my imagination working overtime, I had myself tied in knots. Then Trey and I thrashed out a few things. And he made me realize there are worse answers than the truth; the worst answer is no answer at all. No matter who did this, we have to know."

After a moment, Jason sighed. "Yeah."

Neither one of us was pretending to grieve for Innis. I doubted anyone would, including his wife and son. I know that all I felt about his death was a painful anger—at him, for having driven someone to murder him.

The lousy bastard couldn't even *die* without causing trouble.

Jason didn't seem to have anything else to say. He remained with me until Trey returned a couple of minutes later, then mumbled something about needing coffee—or something stronger—and left us to go downstairs.

Trey touched my back, his big hand rubbing lightly. "You all right?"

"I've been better." I looked up at him and managed a smile. "Is Winslow on his way?"

"Along with the forensic team from my department and the Fulton County medical examiner; Nick is formally requesting our assistance."

"I don't blame him," I offered dryly. "I'll bet there have been only two murders here in the last ten years—and both have happened since yesterday in the same house."

"Something like that," Trey said.

"Yaaaahh."

We both looked around as Choo came toward us from the direction of the stairway, and I bent to pick him up hastily as soon as he reached us. "No, cat, we can't let you go into that room . . ."

"What?" Trey asked when my voice trailed off.

"He flinched." I was holding my cat carefully with one arm while exploring his thick fur with the other hand. As I probed gently along his rib cage, Choo stiffened and growled. "There's a sore place here at his side."

Trey's hand joined mine, deft and quick. "No wound, but there is a tender spot. A bruise, maybe."

"Like somebody hit him with something—or kicked him," I realized. Before I could begin to get indignant about that, Choo turned his head, craning the way cats do, and stared into Innis's room with his nose twitching. That was when I saw the small, brownish flecks on his fur just above his collar on the back of his neck. It was one of the few places Choo had trouble cleaning himself.

"Trey . . . is that what I think it is?" I asked, pointing out the flecks.

Carefully, Trey picked off one of the particles and rubbed it between his finger and thumb. "Blood."

We could both see that Choo had no cut on his neck, and both of us were thinking the same thing. I said it out loud. "I suppose he could have gotten it later, after Innis was killed. The door was closed when we got here, but we don't know if Grace found it open."

"No," Trey agreed. "I think I'll get a sample of the blood, and of his fur, just in case."

Staring into Innis's room with his eyes narrowed,

Choo growled low in his throat, and the tip of his tail jerked in a way any cat owner would recognize.

Choo was royally pissed off.

IT WAS AFTER three before the forensic team from Trey's department and the medical examiner finished their business and left. The body was on its way to Atlanta as well. In the parlor, my extremely tense and unhappy relatives had been fingerprinted and had the stressful awareness of knowing that said prints were also on their way to Atlanta.

Trey and Captain Winslow were alone in the library discussing recent developments before they started to go over the individual statements (two sets of statements now). I was expected to join them there eventually, but found myself lingering in the entrance hall at the doorway of the parlor—probably because I'm a closet masochist or something.

The others were in the parlor. Even Emily, heavy-eyed and listless, was there. From the look of her, she wasn't even aware that anything other than Lawrence's death had occurred. As for Grace, she was still unnaturally calm, sitting bolt upright in a chair and looking at nothing. Peter was white, and so tightly wound that he prowled the room, unable to sit down.

I couldn't read much of anything from the others, except for Vanessa. She was scrubbing at her fingers with a paper towel, trying to get the ink off, and the look she shot me was pure hate. I suppose I'd earned that from her either because I'd brought a cop into the house, or else because I belonged by blood to a family that had produced two murdered bodies in less than twenty-four hours. Or she could have been mad at me because Jason had rejected her.

Yes, I know that isn't rational. Neither was she.

"Why didn't they take *your* fingerprints?" she demanded.

I kept my own voice mild; there was nothing to be gained by stirring her up more than she already was. "My prints are on file."

"Criminal past?" Her high voice was malicious.

"No." I hoped to God nobody'd tell her about the Townsend investigation; I'd never hear the end of that. "I had to register the prints when I got my license."

Still roaming, Peter asked jerkily, "What kind of license?"

It didn't surprise me that he didn't know; we hadn't seen much of each other in recent years, and he was never curious about what other people were doing with their lives.

"Private investigator's license," I replied.

He stopped dead and stared at me. "You're a private eye?"

I winced. Wouldn't you? "I'm a private investigator specializing in the location of lost objects. And people," I said with extreme care, accepting the simplest label even though I don't consider myself a P.I.

"And you're sleeping with a cop? That must be handy," Vanessa observed mockingly.

"Vanessa," Adam said sharply.

I decided I wasn't a masochist after all, because I wasn't enjoying this.

One of Winslow's men was standing in the hall just a couple of feet away from me, not precisely guarding but near enough, and after glancing his way I decided it wasn't going to do much good for me to hover within sight of my relatives. Peter and Vanessa were the only two (now that Innis was gone) who would attack me out loud, but I couldn't help noticing that both Cain and Maddy looked wary. That hurt.

I was about to turn away when Kerry spoke suddenly. Her voice was clear and sure, and she was looking directly at me.

"No matter what, we have to find out the truth. If we don't, the innocent will suffer more than the guilty."

Someone else who agreed with Trey. I sent her a faint smile, feeling grateful, and then made my way to the library. The doors were open, so I just went in, finding Trey and Winslow at the big oak desk that had belonged to Grandfather.

They made an interesting contrast. Winslow was wearing his uniform, of course, every bit as spiffy as before, and the big gun on his hip looked rather intimidating. Trey was as casual as me in jeans and a sweater, with no outward sign that he, too, was a cop.

Winslow was seated behind the desk (the position of authority, a bit of stage management I fully appreciated), while Trey half sat on the desk itself. They were both bent over notes and statements lying on the blotter, Trey impassive and Winslow frowning.

I had the sudden notion that if I'd come in a couple of minutes earlier I would have walked into a disagreement. I could feel the tension in the room, and I was positive Trey wasn't very happy about something. I have to admit, that made me a lot more alert than I'd been, and a little wary.

All I could do for the moment, however, was file the thought away and await developments. That's the hell of casting your lot with the police when you aren't a cop; you're not entitled to any information at all since you aren't officially tied in with the investigation, and nobody mistrusts amateurs more than a dedicated cop with a murder to solve.

I'm talking about Winslow, by the way. Trey was different, and he had a lot of faith in my so-called abilities, but I doubted he'd managed to completely convince Winslow that I could be an asset to the investigation.

"Are you guys ready for me, or should I take a walk?" I asked, coming slowly into the room.

Sighing audibly, Winslow looked at me with grim spaniel eyes. "The only good thing about today," he announced, "is that we have fewer suspects than we had yesterday."

I took that for a yes, and went over to sit in a comfortable chair by the window. "Since your guys took a second set of statements while the forensic team was here, I assume a number of us were ruled out. Who's left?"

Winslow shuffled through his papers and produced one, frowning down at it. "We have eight people with shaky or unverifiable alibis for the time we believe Innis Langdon was killed."

"Cross off Kerry and Baxter," I said.

"Why?" Winslow demanded, frowning at me now. "I'm suspicious on principle when a husband and wife alibi each other—and in this case, she claims to have been asleep the whole time. He says they were together in their suite until after nine-thirty, and then he left for a morning run. And their rooms were right down the hall from Langdon's."

I noticed the hick of yesterday had been cast off; his voice was sharp and incisive, and his expression could best be described as extremely intelligent.

I shrugged, holding his gaze steadily. "Look, you

wanted me in here to keep you from chasing down blind alleys. I'm telling you that's what you'll find if you seriously consider either Kerry or Baxter. Neither one of them did it. Period.''

His eyes narrowed. ''They're family. How do I know you won't do your best to protect your family, Miss Montana?''

''You don't.'' I let that sink in for a moment, glancing aside to see Trey's slight smile, then returned my attention to Winslow. ''You also have no reason to trust my word. All I can tell you is that I'll give you a truthful answer—and an honest opinion. And, in case you're not sure, even a bleeding heart like me has a hard time swallowing two murders in less than twenty-four hours, both inside my own family. I want to know what the hell happened as badly as you do.''

Winslow stared at me for a long moment, then nodded and said briskly, ''Fair enough. For the time being, then, I'll cross off Mr. and Mrs. Hart. That leaves us with six.''

I didn't hesitate. ''Cain and Maddy, Peter, Vanessa, Grace, and Emily. Grace was with Emily, who was sedated, so you only have Grace's word she was there—directly across the hall from where her hateful husband was killed. What about the others?''

Trey answered me, his tone dispassionate. ''Peter says he was in his bedroom, alone. He had coffee sent up around eight—that's been verified—and claims he didn't know anything had happened until I went up after eleven to tell him about his father.''

I hadn't envied him that job, for which he had volunteered. ''Vanessa?''

''She had coffee sent up at about the same time. Then she remained in her suite until past nine-thirty, when she came downstairs to the breakfast room.'' Trey was looking at me steadily.

I knew what he was thinking, and said it out loud. ''She's been here in the house for more than a week, ever since she followed Mother and Adam over from England. Has the staff verified that her usual habit is to have breakfast—late—in her room?''

''Yeah, they have,'' Winslow said. ''Today was the first time anyone's seen her up before ten. And the maid who served her coffee says she was fully dressed at eight o'clock. That's a striking change in her usual habits.''

Trying my best to be fair despite my opinion of my stepsis, I said, ''Well, she could have had trouble sleeping after yesterday. Maybe that explains the change.''

Neither man commented on that. Winslow consulted his notes again, and said, ''Cain and Maddy Buford were served breakfast in their suite at eight forty-five. Each of them claims the other never left those rooms until Trey knocked on their door after eleven.''

Now, *that* rang a definite false note, much as I hated to think it. Okay, maybe their usual habits had been upset by Lawrence's death—but I couldn't remember anything ever keeping Cain and Maddy from their morning walk.

I looked up to find both men watching me steadily, and offered a flat opinion. ''Maddy couldn't kill anybody.''

''What about Cain?'' Trey asked quietly.

I could hear the damning words echo in my memory, words I'd said to Trey—was it only hours ago? That poison wouldn't have been Cain's way. A gun or knife, maybe. Or beating Innis to a pulp.

Goddamn it.

Reluctantly, I said, "There would have had to be a very, very good reason. Cain's put up with Innis for years; why suddenly snap and bash him? Besides—if Cain had killed Lawrence by accident, he would have been too horrified by the mistake to go through with the second murder. That's my opinion."

"All right," Winslow said. "What about Grace Langdon?"

I noticed he didn't cross off Cain's name. Or Maddy's.

Looking across the room at nothing, I tried to bring Grace into focus. In a way, it was as difficult as trying to visualize Lawrence. Negative people, both of them. One had been bland and the other was . . .

"Faded," I muttered to myself. "All the color squeezed out of her." Then I blinked at the two men and shook my head. "She's never stood up to Innis that I can remember. I suppose she could have snapped—but I don't think she would have been able to kill Innis after Lawrence."

Winslow looked down at his list for a moment, then back at me. "You didn't offer any opinions on Peter Langdon or Vanessa Rowland."

"About Peter, I just don't know. He's been more than usually volatile this weekend, but . . . I know he scares easily, and Lawrence's death would have frightened him badly—especially once he knew Trey was a cop." I shrugged, aware of something tapping at the back of my mind but unable to grasp it. "Vanessa. Well, I've only just met her, and she hasn't—I hope—shown to advantage this weekend. I'm sure Trey told you about our conversation regarding her this morning?"

"Yeah, he did."

"Then you already know my opinion. If Innis insulted her, she might have dropped poison into his glass. From what she said this morning, it's obvious she considered Lawrence the next best thing to nonexistent, so she might have dismissed his death and gone after Innis again. Who knows?"

Winslow sighed. "You'd think with maids going up and down the stairs all morning, one of them would have noticed something helpful, but no. They didn't see anybody except the people they served."

"It's a big house," I offered.

Almost glaring at me, the county cop said, "No shit."

I couldn't really blame him for being a mite testy. I wasn't terribly happy myself. "Look, wasn't there anything in the room that might help?"

Winslow glanced up at Trey, then back at me, and I felt even more alert. Damn it, there *was* something they weren't telling me. I tried very hard to keep my face relatively blank, and listened to what the good captain deigned to tell me.

(Yes, I know I was bristling. Put yourself in my place. Wouldn't you?)

"We're reasonably sure your cat was in the room at some point. We don't have verification from the lab yet, but the blood on the underside of that newspaper had a few fine hairs sticking in it, and they look like the samples Trey took from, uh, Choo." He paused, then asked, "What do you think of that?"

If I'd been feeling flippant, I might have said Choo wasn't tall enough to have bashed Innis. I was, however, concentrating too hard to feel flippant.

"Well, he didn't get into the room while Innis was alive, that's for sure. There's no way Innis would have sat there calmly reading his paper with Choo in the room; he would have chased him out. And Choo got blood on his coat, so—if it was Innis's blood—it must have been after the murder. I suppose he could have followed somebody into the room, either because it was someone he liked, or because his interest was caught by what was happening in the room."

"Smelled blood?" Winslow suggested.

"Maybe. He doesn't like blood, though. He won't eat raw liver, and once when I cut my hand in the kitchen he ran away from me." I frowned, brooding. "He might have followed somebody into the room just before Innis was killed, then panicked when he smelled the blood. Somebody hit or kicked him—maybe in that room, and maybe because whoever it was couldn't catch him to carry him out. He could have run under the newspaper then, and that's how he got the blood on his coat—and the hairs on the newspaper."

"Pity he can't talk," Winslow muttered.

I glanced at Trey, both of us remembering when he'd said the same thing about Choo during the Townsend investigation.

"Okay," Winslow said with a sigh. "We'll have to get the six of them in here one by one, and see if we can shake anything loose. Until the lab and autopsy results come in, all we've got are the statements and the question of motive and opportunity."

I didn't believe him. He had something else, or thought he did. And, whatever it was, I was pretty sure Trey knew about it as well, and that they'd decided—or Winslow had—not to tell me for the time being.

The forensic team. They must have found something at the murder scene. But what? Something pointing to a specific individual? The lab results weren't back yet, so it had to be a fairly obvious piece of evidence that didn't need to be examined or interpreted. Damn it . . .

It made me extremely nervous.

I cleared my throat. "Mind if I suggest that you question Peter first?"

"Why?"

"Because if he has to wait much longer, he's going to go completely to pieces and end up sedated like Emily. He won't be much good to you then."

After an exchange of glances between the two men, Trey went to fetch Peter. Choo came into the room in the meantime, sparing Winslow no more than a glance before climbing up into my lap and making himself comfortable.

Watching me absently stroke my cat, Winslow said, "After last night, I figured you'd tell me to go to hell in a hurry if I asked for your help again. So this is a surprise. What brought you over to our side?"

I looked at him and shrugged. "A lot of agonizing," I answered. "And Trey. By the way—you'll get more out of Peter if you don't use the hick routine. Authority scares him more than subtlety."

Nick Winslow smiled slightly, but all he said was "Gotcha."

When my cousin came into the room a couple of minutes later, I couldn't help but feel a stab of sympathy. He really did look like hell, with dark circles under his unnaturally brilliant eyes and a sickly pallor. I could almost smell his fear, and it was certainly visible.

He threw a quick, faintly betrayed look at me, then perched uneasily on the edge of the chair Nick had placed squarely in front of the desk. Trey settled into a chair on the other side of the desk from me, which placed the three of us in positions facing Peter.

Winslow took it easy on him at first, simply going over both his statements point by point, quite mildly. I watched Peter, trying to look for signs—and was a little surprised when I realized he was more jumpy about what had happened the previous day than the day of his father's murder.

"You left the house yesterday morning, did you not, Mr. Langdon?"

"I, uh, borrowed Trey's car, yes. I wanted to get out of the house for a while, that's all. So I drove into Atlanta."

The car, I thought. There was something about the car . . .

"What did you do in Atlanta?"

"I went to a movie. Since it was Saturday, there were morning shows, you know. Then I drove around some more and—and came back here."

Winslow continued taking him through the day step by step, and I watched a little of his nervousness fade. He seemed genuinely astonished that Lawrence had died, and made haste to say he wouldn't have known where to find any rat poison even if he'd been looking for it.

He tensed up again when Winslow went over his second statement, and for a while there I couldn't pin down his uneasiness.

"You had coffee sent up to your room, Mr. Langdon?"

"Yes. Around eight o'clock, I think. And I didn't leave the room until Trey came."

"That was more than three hours, Mr. Langdon. What did you do all that time?"

"Nothing. Oh—I had a book. I read."

"You didn't see or talk to anyone?"

"No, I told you. I was alone." He hesitated, then asked a bit jerkily, "Do you know when—I mean, exactly when—it happened?"

Winslow studied him for a moment, then said, "We think between nine and nine-thirty."

For an instant, Peter looked blank. But then, clear as day, I saw relief in his eyes. Before anyone else could speak, I did.

"Who were you with, Peter?"

Peter looked at me, then at Trey and Winslow, then back at me. And his eyes were pleading. "He didn't lie to me, did he, Lane? That is when it happened?"

Any doubts I might have had as to Peter's possible guilt vanished. Gently, I said, "No, he didn't lie. Who were you with?"

"Mom." He slumped in his chair, still shaky but enormously relieved. "I—I lied on the statement. I was upset, and wanted to talk to Mom, so I slipped down to the second floor a little after eight-thirty. I didn't think Mom would be in the suite with Dad, because she always left early, but I saw one of the maids take a tray to the room across the hall—Emily's room—and heard Mom's voice. I stayed out of sight—"

"Why?" Winslow demanded.

Peter flushed vividly. "Oh—the way it looked, a grown man running to his mama. Hell, I don't know, I just didn't want the maid to see me. So, when she'd gone, I tapped on Emily's door, and Mom came out. She said Emily'd taken her pills and was asleep, but she didn't want to leave her alone too long. We went back upstairs to my room."

"For how long?"

Eagerly now, Peter said, "It was more than an hour, because Mom looked at her watch and said she had to get back to Emily since she'd been left alone more than an hour. So we were together from before nine until nearly ten."

Winslow had a great poker face; I couldn't tell if he believed Peter or not. He just grunted, checked the details on the remainder of the statement, and dismissed my cousin.

When we were alone again, he said, "If those two alibi each other, and Mrs. Langdon says Mrs. Stoddard was knocked out by sedatives, we've just ruled out three more. Why the hell couldn't that kid come clean in the beginning?"

"He was worried about his mother," I offered. "If Innis had been killed earlier or later than he was, Grace would have been a heavy favorite. She was directly across the hall, and her companion was a sedated woman."

"He suspected his own mother?" Winslow said.

"Guilty consciences are funny things," I said. "If you feel guilty yourself, it's very easy to see possible guilt in someone else."

Winslow leaned back in his chair and stared at me. "What did he have to feel guilty about, if he didn't kill his father or Stoddard?"

I'd been sitting there putting a few things together in my mind, and looked at Trey. "Remember yesterday, out on the veranda when Peter came back? He was acting so cheerful, and you said he was trying too hard?"

"I remember. I went inside to talk to him, but within minutes after I joined him, he came up with some vague excuse and went upstairs."

"And last night, when Lawrence died, Peter was just

about frozen with shock. Later, in the parlor, he actually laughed—a bit hysterically, I thought. It must have scared the hell out of him when it became obvious Lawrence had been murdered, because I'm willing to bet Peter had made up his mind that morning to do something crazy. Maybe—kill his father."

Winslow blinked at me. "Wait a minute, now. He planned to do it—but didn't?"

I smiled slightly. "You have to understand, Peter's very high-strung, and more than a little childish in many ways. Innis kept the reins tight. Yesterday morning, when Peter asked to borrow Trey's car, he was about as angry as I'd ever seen him. According to Wanda, he'd even tried to hit his father the day before. He said something to me about forcing Innis to take him seriously. Then he left the house. I think he had some wild plan to buy a gun."

Winslow consulted his papers with a frown, then said, "His home is in northern Florida; he couldn't legally buy a gun in Georgia."

"I doubt he even thought of that. Not that it mattered, in the end. I bet he'll always be grateful it was Trey's car he borrowed."

Trey got it then, and nodded. To me, he said, "Of course. The police radio."

"Uh huh. With, as I remember, a neat little yellow sticker that says property of Atlanta P.D. Peter realized you were a cop. And he must have nearly had a heart attack at the thought of shooting his father with you in the house. Talk about the cold rush of sanity. He was completely different when he got back here, and he stayed as far away from Innis as he could from then on. Remember how, last night, Jase and I both decided that

Peter was acting scared? I'll bet that's it, Trey—and it's just like Peter.''

After a moment, Winslow searched through his papers and produced one, which he read carefully. "His mother claims she was in Mrs. Stoddard's room until just before eleven, when she crossed the hall and found her husband dead. Why didn't she mention spending more than an hour with her son? The same reason? Because she thought him being on the second floor during that time might make him a likelier suspect?''

"Probably," I agreed. "Other than the three of us and Jason, none of my relatives has any knowledge of the approximate time of death. As far as they're concerned, the entire morning is treacherous.''

So Winslow talked to Grace next, and he didn't bother going over her statement. He merely said, "We believe your husband died between nine and nine-thirty this morning, Mrs. Langdon. Where were you during that time?''

Grace, still unnaturally calm, looked at him with huge, faded green eyes, sighed just a little, and quietly verified Peter's revised statement. They had been together in his room.

I didn't offer an opinion on that, and neither did Trey or Winslow. Vanessa was next, and she came into the room with a flounce, demanding to know why "we" were being subjected to all these endless questions.

Winslow soothed her apologetically—and I have to admit, he was good at it. His drawl would have stretched a city block, his smile was ingratiating, and he looked at her with puppy-dog eyes filled with simple admiration. It was patently obvious he thought her the classiest lady to ever cross his path.

Vanessa fell for it.

In an "Aw, shucks" tone filled with respectful "ma'ams," Winslow went over her statements, slowly and methodically. Minute by minute, Vanessa relaxed, her smile superior and scornful, her verification of each point haughty and slightly bored.

I must say, I enjoyed those few minutes. Mean of me, I know, but I didn't like Vanessa. And I don't care how good a person you are, it's simple human nature to view with pleasure the anticipated Waterloo of someone you dislike.

When he finished going over her statements, Winslow sat back and gazed at her in silence for a long moment. The puppy-dog eyes slowly hardened, and his smile became just as scornful as hers. His drawl remained, but derision replaced the respect.

"Ma'am, are you sure these statements are accurate?"

"Of course," she replied, nose lifting.

"You had absolutely no reason to injure or kill Innis Langdon and, in fact, barely knew him?"

"I've told you that, Captain," she snapped.

Winslow folded his hands over her statements, and continued to regard her steadily. "It might interest you to know, Miss Rowland, that we believe the poison ingested by Lawrence Stoddard was intended for Innis Langdon. The glasses might easily have been switched at some point. A number of fingerprints were found on the glass containing the poison. Since you were . . . kind enough . . . to get a refill for Mr. Langdon last night, one of those prints could be yours."

I gave him full marks for not stating definitely that Vanessa's prints had been found when he didn't know they had; he wasn't about to make the mistake of lying outright in order to rattle her. A good defense attorney could use that kind of mistake to his advantage.

Vanessa looked less scornful once her mind sorted through the information. She wasn't smart, but I thought she had a lively sense of self-preservation.

"So?" she demanded finally, her eyes shifting nervously away from Winslow's stare. "I hardly knew either of them, and I certainly didn't have a reason to kill Innis."

"Didn't you?" Winslow asked very softly.

He waited, immovable, a certain deadly patience in his total lack of expression. It was extremely effective. Even I felt my nerves stretch as the silence dragged on, and I didn't have reason to be worried.

Well, not much anyway.

Vanessa looked like a rabbit hypnotized by a hawk. Her eyes grew larger, her body seemed to draw in on itself, and she wet her lips nervously.

With perfect timing, Winslow said in the same soft voice, "Isn't it true, Miss Rowland, that you did have a reason? Isn't it true that you were sexually involved with Mr. Langdon? Isn't it true that he . . . visited . . . your room yesterday morning before lunchtime?"

EIGHT

IF SHE'D BEEN smarter, she would simply have said, "No, it isn't true," and dared him to prove it if he could. She wasn't smart, though. And she had a lousy poker face, even worse than mine.

Slack-jawed shock. Not surprise, but fear of the oh-my-God-you-know variety.

"I—I don't—I don't know what you're talking about," she stuttered.

"Of course you do, Miss Rowland. It was such an exciting secret, wasn't it? With his wife and your own father in the same house?"

"No! No, I wouldn't—I'd never—"

"Mr. Langdon seems to have been rather well-known for his effect on women, and his sexual habits. He always made a play for blonds. Especially younger women."

The maids talked, I thought. And since at least two of them had been at the house for several years—and since both were blonds—they'd probably had quite a lot to say about horny old Innis.

"What happened, Miss Rowland? What did he do to make you angry? Did he use you? Did he laugh at you

163

when you wanted to continue the relationship—or more? Did he push you away and call you a silly little bitch? Is that why you decided to kill him?''

I think that it was the remorseless scorn in Winslow's voice more than the accusation of guilt in a murder that finally got to Vanessa. He was looking at her as if he saw a cheap slut, and even the dumbest woman alive would have recognized his contempt.

Watching her face crack was an awful sight. It made me feel a little sick. As young as she was, the only thing holding Vanessa together was her vanity; when Winslow painted a flat picture of an amoral whore and stared at her with distaste, it hit her hard. I suppose it was even worse because he was an authority figure, and because there was really no defense she could offer for her behavior.

I couldn't look away from her, much as I wanted to.

Dry-eyed and haggard, she looked older than any woman her age had a right to. And her voice was very dull when she finally responded to the accusation.

''I didn't kill him. And I didn't want an affair. It—it was casual for me, too. He hit on me and—and I'd never had a man that old. It was just that one time, in my room. I didn't kill him. I didn't.''

After a moment, Winslow said, ''You can go, Miss Rowland. For now.''

She almost felt her way out of the room, like somebody who was suddenly blind.

I was looking down at Choo, stroking him steadily. ''Does Adam have to know about that?'' I heard myself ask. I still felt fairly neutral about my new stepfather, but even if I'd hated him I would have asked that question. No man should hear such things about his daughter.

"Not unless it proves relevant to the case." Winslow's voice was a bit harsh.

I glanced over at him briefly. He looked like a man who had bitten down hard on something that tasted really bad. I didn't know if it was because of what Vanessa was—or what he'd done to her.

"I'll see Emily Stoddard next," he announced.

That interview was brief and far less painful. He was questioning Emily for the first time (because she'd been sedated yesterday), but he didn't get much out of her at all. She teared up the moment he mentioned Lawrence's name, and kept murmuring over and over, "Who would want to kill my Larry?" As for Innis's death, she merely looked at Winslow blankly and shook her head when he asked her the usual questions.

Finally, giving up in the face of her incoherence, he dismissed her.

"Maddy Buford," he said.

Choo was tense in my lap, not purring, and I knew he was feeling my own tension. This was it, I thought. Winslow had a look I recognized, the look of a confident man missing only one piece of the puzzle.

And he expected to find that piece any minute now.

All I could do was wait. It's not my favorite activity at the best of times, and I was hardly in the mood for it that day, but I didn't have much choice.

Maddy was very calm, very composed, when she came into the room. I watched her face as Winslow went over her statements—and I couldn't read a thing in her serene expression.

That scared me.

She didn't fidget or avoid his eyes. She didn't look at Trey or me, yet she didn't seem to be ignoring us; it was just that all her attention was focused completely on Winslow. Her replies to the big cop across the desk were simple, polite, and wholly unrevealing.

"Yes, Captain, that's right."

"No, Captain, neither my husband nor I left our rooms at all this morning."

"No, Captain, I had no reason to kill Innis."

Winslow was drawling as he questioned her, but he must have realized she was no fool because he didn't attempt to charm her or appear overly innocent. I had the feeling he was weighing her, trying to decide how best to elicit the information he so clearly wanted from her.

Finally, after going over both her statements, he sat back and looked at her. In a direct and matter-of-fact voice, he asked, "Mrs. Buford, why did you slap Innis Langdon out in front of the house early yesterday evening?"

Maddy didn't waste time denying a scene that someone had clearly witnessed. She merely replied quite readily in an equally matter-of-fact voice, "Because he said something offensive to me, Captain. I suppose I should have been accustomed to his ways after so many years, but I was not in the best of moods at the time and reacted before I could control myself."

"What did he say to you, ma'am?"

"I would prefer not to repeat it, Captain."

"And if I insist, Mrs. Buford?"

Gently, she said, "Then I will refuse, Captain. Under oath, I must, of course, comply. But this is not a courtroom. And it's my judgment that what Innis said to me yesterday evening has absolutely no bearing on your investigation."

Winslow must have realized he was a bit hamstrung. He could insist until he was blue in the face, but it was obvious Maddy would continue to refuse. Moreover, her gentle nature was so palpable that it would have taken an absolute monster to make any attempt to break down her resistance.

He'd been able to do that to Vanessa, partly because he felt a genuine distaste for her morals. But Maddy was completely different—and he knew it.

"Thank you, Mrs. Buford," he said after a moment. "Would you ask your husband to come in here, please?"

"Of course, Captain." As graceful as Choo on his best days, she strolled from the room.

Winslow tugged at his tie and muttered, "Damnit." But there was a certain bright anticipation in his eyes as he watched the doorway.

It created an awful feeling in the pit of my stomach. Cain. Winslow thought it was Cain. Even more, he'd made up his mind that it was Cain. Cain had been the bartender last night, with the perfect opportunity to slip something into one of the glasses, and he and Maddy alibied each other for the entire morning today. An alibi provided by a loving wife was an alibi many juries could easily discount.

If, of course, there was evidence against the husband to prove guilt beyond a reasonable doubt.

I was scared. My various stepfathers had passed through my life so briefly that none had made much of an impression: Grandfather and Cain had been the only real father figures in my life since I was ten years old. I had loved Grandfather very much. I had adored Cain.

He had put me on my first pony. He had opened my eyes and my mind to the wonder of life, by allowing me to assist him at the birth of numerous foals and calves. He had built me a hope chest, working in secret during one long winter to make it a thing of beauty and craftsmanship. With the stark realities of the hardships and daily struggle of ranching, he had taught me the important lesson that life is precious because it is wrestled always from death.

And they had always *been* there, he and Maddy, a granite core of stability and emotional support throughout Mother's arrivals and departures in my life. I still ran to them and the safety of Wyoming when I was troubled or in pain, and was always welcomed and soothed by their love and confidence in me.

I couldn't run to them now. And, when this was over, I didn't know if I'd be welcome there.

I made myself look at Cain when he came in, feeling a pang when he didn't even glance at me. While Winslow calmly and methodically went over his statements, I watched my uncle, worried and afraid.

He was relaxed, unruffled. His deep voice was mild, his replies to all the questions polite but firm. He gave virtually the same answers Maddy had, denying that he had any reason at all to have wanted Innis dead.

I was watching Cain so intently that I didn't realize a new element had been added until I heard Winslow's question.

"What is this, Mr. Buford?"

Without hesitating or, apparently, feeling even a twinge of nervousness, Cain replied, "That, Captain, is a cuff link. It belongs to me."

I looked quickly at Winslow. He had produced a small plastic bag that had apparently been in a drawer of the desk, and it contained one cuff link that I recognized. A bit flashy, it was made of gold and onyx, with the gold monogram clearly visible.

I had given it to Cain on his birthday five years before.

God, talk about irony.

Winslow's voice was flat. "When did you last wear it, Mr. Buford?"

"I'm afraid I can't remember."

His mouth tightening, Winslow said, "Can you explain the fact that it was found in Innis Langdon's room this morning?"

"No."

Winslow set the cuff link on the center of the desk, shuffled through the papers before him, and produced one. He apparently read it, silently, then looked at Cain.

"You had an argument late last night with Mr. Langdon. What was that argument about?"

I looked quickly at Cain's face, finding it completely unreadable. And his voice was the same.

"No argument with Innis was ever *about* anything, Captain. Anyone who knew him will tell you that much. He loved the sound of his own voice, especially raised to a shout."

"Why did you go to his sitting room after midnight?"

Cain shrugged.

Winslow stared at him for a long moment, then said softly, "What had he done to your wife, Mr. Buford?"

Cain went utterly white, and his eyes glittered. He wasn't shocked or afraid. He was in the grip of a fury so deadly I could actually feel it emanating from him.

No. Oh, God, please . . . no . . .

At least a minute must have passed before Cain smiled thinly, his rage under control. "I don't know what you're talking about, Captain," he said pleasantly.

"We'll find out, Mr. Buford," Winslow told him in a voice of complete confidence. "One way or another."

Cain didn't react or respond in any way to the threat. "May I go now?" he asked politely.

"Don't leave the grounds."

"I wouldn't think of it." Cain rose and left the room unhurriedly. He still didn't look at me.

I'm not terribly good at sitting calmly when my nerves are jagged. And they were definitely jagged. I set Choo on the floor and got up, wandering a few feet to stand looking at the books on the shelves. It was a familiar room to me, a comfortable room. Or had been.

It was funny. Since Trey and I had arrived, I had been looking at the house and everything in it as if it were unconnected to me. I hadn't been haunted by memories—good or bad. Even the night before, when I'd told Trey about my father leaving, there had been no pictures in my mind associating what I was remembering with the house.

Everything was familiar—yet it didn't mean anything to me. I hadn't thought about it before, but now I knew why that was so. This place had stopped being home to me when I was ten years old. After that, it was just a house I lived in sometimes, and after I grew up, it was only a place I visited.

For me, "home" had become a Wyoming ranch in the summertime. It had been the only safe place I'd known after that, the only place where there had been no abrupt and unsettling changes to hurt or frighten a child.

A place where I'd never lost anyone.

For several long moments, as I stood there in that silent room, what I felt most was a sharp grief for the loss of that place. It could never be a haven for me again.

Whatever was going on between Maddy and Cain, they had shut me out completely; I wasn't on *their* side because I'd thrown in my lot with the police. It was obvious they wouldn't trust me with any damaging information—because they couldn't be sure I wouldn't use it against them.

Oh, yeah, it hurt. Even if all this turned out well (and, God, I hoped it would), my relationship with them would never be the same again. Maybe the wounds could be healed, with time. Eventually, Cain and Maddy would probably understand, and forgive, the choice I'd made. But we had trusted each other unconditionally . . . and that was gone forever.

I'd never be able to forget that I had wondered—if only for a brief time—if the uncle I adored was capable of murder; they would never be able to forget that I had chosen to help look for the truth no matter what the cost.

I'm sure the silence in the room lasted no more than a few minutes while I grappled with a part of that cost. In the end, of course, all I could do was pay the price and go on. I could hardly go back and change anything. My only way now was to push ahead, and try and make sure the cost wasn't too high for everyone involved.

"Who's the witness?" I asked without turning to face the two men.

"Alexander," Trey answered me quietly. "He promised Elizabeth he would check on Emily during the night, and when he went to do that, he overheard part of an argument between Cain and Innis. He said his impression was that Innis had done something to Maddy. Cain threatened to kill him."

I somehow knew that Trey had been the one to get that out of Alexander at some point today, and I believed it. There had been an argument between Cain and Innis. That didn't surprise me at all. But, in general, people who threaten—out loud—to kill someone don't follow through, and in any case I was positive Cain hadn't.

I might have doubted him momentarily, but that uncertainty hadn't lasted long.

I turned around finally, leaning back against the shelves and sliding my hands into my pockets. I looked at Winslow, even though Trey had spoken. "So? Nearly everyone in this house has threatened to kill him. I admit I've felt the urge a few times myself."

Flatly, with each word bitten off, Winslow said, "Cain Buford was the bartender last night; he had every opportunity to poison a drink, and no one would have noticed. He went to Langdon's room hours later after the police had gone, had a violent argument with him, and was heard by a witness threatening to kill him for having in some way injured Mrs. Buford. His only alibi for the entire morning is his wife."

My mind wasn't in very good shape, but I felt compelled to try and punch holes in Winslow's neat little theory. And when you're not sure you'll have much—if any—evidence to back you up, sarcasm works wonders.

"Oh, I see. For whatever reason, he tried to kill Innis—and got Lawrence by mistake. Then, ignoring the presence of a homicide detective in the house, he went to Innis's room, had a screaming match with him—and then waited more than eight hours to bash him over the head. It apparently didn't occur to him that it wasn't real smart to kill a man when he was already under suspicion for another murder. Nice try, Captain, but my uncle isn't a fool.''

The derision in my voice had an effect. Winslow started getting mad. ''Neither am I, Miss Montana,'' he snapped. ''So far, Cain Buford is the best suspect I've got for both murders. Unless, that is, you can pull a convenient homicidal maniac out of your hat.''

I wished I could. God, did I wish I could.

''You don't have any proof,'' I said flatly. ''That cuff link must have been lost last night, because I doubt Cain got all dressed up today to commit murder. Since none of us planned to go to church, you may have noticed he's wearing a sweater. He dressed more formally last night because we all do for dinner. Maybe he lost the cuff link then, but Innis didn't die then, did he? So you can't call it proof that Cain was in Innis's room any time after last night. You can't place him at the scene anywhere near the time of the murder.''

My voice held steady. I don't know how I managed it, but I did.

''He had a violent argument with Langdon,'' Winslow said. ''Langdon had done something to injure Mrs. Buford—''

''That's hearsay. And it's like carting water to the ocean; we've *all* had arguments with Innis. Quite a few this weekend alone. You have no proof at all there was a motive for Cain to have killed him.''

''No?'' Winslow was staring at me grimly. ''Did you see his face when I brought it up? He was so furious he could have killed right then.''

''Are you going to take that to court?'' I demanded. ''Your opinion that he was angry? A cuff link he wasn't wearing the day a murder was committed? A glass with a hell of a lot of prints on it—even if one of them is

his? He was the bartender, for Christ's sake; his prints
are on *all* the glasses.''

Winslow was definitely mad now. He didn't like being questioned, especially by—and this was obvious—
a lowly P.I. who was, at best, an amateur when it came
to murder investigations. And most especially when she
was defending one of her own relatives.

"There is a motive," he snapped, "and I'm going
to find it. I'll question everyone in this house a dozen
times if I have to; sooner or later, someone will remember seeing or hearing that motive. Maddy Buford
may not crack—she's the kind that doesn't—but Cain
Buford will. Eventually.''

I walked over to the desk and put my hands on it,
leaning forward to stare at him. "Even if you find what
you believe is a motive, you have nothing but circumstantial evidence—and damned little of that. There
weren't any prints on the figurine, were there? The
prints on the glass don't mean a damned thing, and you
know it. Prints on the doorknob of Innis's room? So
what—Cain was there last night and nobody's tried to
deny it. If he wanted to murder Innis, why not do it
then when he was supposedly furious?''

"Because Mrs. Langdon was in the next room!"
Winslow almost bellowed—then froze suddenly, his
eyes abruptly speculative.

Oh, shit, I thought.

"She might have overheard the argument," he muttered.

"You've got a one-track mind," I said coldly.
"Haven't you been listening to me? There are motives
all over the place, they don't mean a damned thing.
You don't have any evidence. And even if *you* don't
happen to believe it, Cain does have an alibi.''

"His wife's word," Winslow scoffed.

I straightened. "Yeah, well, you let any prosecutor spend five minutes with Maddy and see if he wants to attack her word in court in front of a jury."

I could see that made an impression on Winslow, but he was stubbornly convinced Cain was guilty, and was not yet prepared to back down. If he could find a motive strong enough, and if none of the scanty physical evidence ruled Cain out, then my uncle would be arrested for murder.

"You haven't eliminated other suspects," I went on flatly. "Vanessa doesn't have an alibi."

"She's a bad liar," he said, shuffling through his papers until he located the statement he wanted. "I doubt very much that she killed him."

The hell of it was, I thought he was probably right. But I wasn't sure. The only thing I was sure of was that Cain wasn't guilty.

Making a last attempt, I said, "You don't even have the medical examiner's report on Innis or Lawrence yet, and you're basing all your assumptions on an *estimated* time of death for Innis. I may not be a cop, but I'll bet you a year's salary the M.E. won't place the time of death within a half-hour period. Innis had been dead at least three hours by the time the M.E. arrived here; no medical authority is going to fix the time of death that precisely—and swear to it in court—when he didn't have immediate access to the body."

I knew what I was saying. Widening the span of time during which Innis *could* have died would mean that a number of alibis wouldn't hold up—probably including those of my mother, stepfather, and brother. It was a risk for me to even suggest such a thing, yes, but I felt sure that as long as Winslow had a number of legitimate suspects he had to consider, he was less likely to make a hasty arrest.

Time. I needed time to try and make sense of this *mess*.

Eyes narrowed, Winslow stared at me. "That may be, Miss Montana, but until I have an official time of death, I'll stick with the estimate. Cain Buford will remain at the top of my list unless and until the *facts* rule him out." Ignoring me now, he looked at Trey. "I need to talk to Mrs. Langdon again. She may have heard something last night."

I'd been on the point of telling Winslow something I'd just remembered, but decided then to hell with it. Let him find out himself.

Trey had remained silent throughout my "conversation" with his friend, and didn't speak when he rose to get Grace for another round of questions. I didn't speak either. I just walked out of the room and headed toward the rear of the house.

I had to get out of there. I had to.

Was I mad at Trey? No, I wasn't. He wasn't in charge of the investigation; Winslow was. And where Trey would quite likely have told me ahead of time about the cuff link and the argument if he'd been in charge (or even if we'd had a moment alone), Winslow had been too pleased with his "evidence" to want to share it with an amateur.

All right, you've probably figured out by now that I was bristling a bit at being regarded as a neophyte. In fact, I was mad about it. As much as I denied being a private investigator, I *did* serve an apprenticeship and take the damned test in order to get my license, and I am not stupid.

Maybe I wasn't very objective, either, but my belief

in Cain's innocence wasn't just loyalty. I was certain he hadn't killed Innis—for a very good reason. Unfortunately, I doubted a jury would understand my argument.

The one possible eyewitness to Innis's murder was my cat. I was willing to bet the lab would verify that Choo had been in that room during or after the murder, and I felt certain that either he had followed the killer in or else had gotten in as that person was about to leave (he regards open doors as blatant invitations). And either the killer hadn't wanted Choo left in there, or else my cat had panicked at the smell of blood and it had seemed prudent to get him out of the room quickly.

Maybe the killer hadn't wanted the body discovered so soon, and knew the howls of an upset Siamese cat would eventually summon someone to the room. It certainly would have. No matter how large the house, a tense Siamese has no trouble at all making himself heard.

Anyway, the point was that in getting Choo out of the room, the killer had kicked him or hit him with something. (Yes, I was assuming it had happened then, mostly because I was reasonably sure that Choo wouldn't have let anyone who was likely to hit him—such as Innis, Vanessa, or maybe Peter—get close enough unless he was panicked.)

Now, if those assumptions were accurate (a big if, I agree, but *if*), there was no way it was Cain. I'd watched him handle animals for more than twenty years and had never seen him strike a single one despite provocation that would have maddened me. No matter how angry or upset Cain might have been, he would never have hurt my cat.

Yeah, I know. A jury would say that a man who had

just committed a murder wouldn't balk at kicking a cat.
They didn't know Cain.

I did.

With no real destination in mind, I was wandering
toward the back of the house, and met Peter in the
solarium. He was whistling softly when he saw me, and
broke off with a guilty expression that was perfectly
understandable. Not especially nice, sounding so
cheerful with your murdered father hardly cold.

"Hi, Lane," he said a bit warily.

I stopped, barely aware of Choo wreathing around
my ankles the way he does when he'd rather be somewhere else. What I *did* notice was that my cat didn't
seem pissed off at Peter, and since Choo can hold a
grudge for a long time, I doubted my cousin had been
the one to kick my cat.

I was, for the moment, discounting alibis, so he could
have done it, all other things being equal. However, the
one thing I was convinced of was that one person had
committed both murders (I wasn't willing to believe
there were two killers in my family), and I couldn't see
Peter's nerve holding up under the strain. Especially if
I'd been right about him experiencing a cold rush of
sanity by discovering that Trey was a cop.

"Peter, where were you planning to go yesterday
morning when you left here?"

He looked startled, then nervous. "You know, Lane.
I told that cop. I went to a movie."

I kept my voice as quiet and unthreatening as I could
manage. "That isn't what I asked you. Where were you
planning to go when you left?"

Peter shrugged jerkily.

Since I doubted he'd blurt out the truth, and since
this was for me rather than a statement, I quit beating

around the bush. "You were going to buy a gun, weren't you, Peter?"

He went white. "I didn't!"

"I know you didn't. Driving Trey's car changed your mind, didn't it? You saw the police radio." After a tense pause, I said, "Come on, Peter—nobody was shot. And you were with your mother when Innis was killed, weren't you?"

"Then it doesn't matter, does it?" he said quickly.

"For my own peace of mind, it does. Look, I'm supposed to be an observant private investigator, and I need confirmation of one of my observations. You were mad as hell when you left here, and almost painfully cheerful when you came back; that was my observation. I think you had a bad scare, and it was finding out Trey was a cop. Yes or no?"

He shifted his weight from foot to foot, then shrugged again. "All right—yes. So what? I thought if I got a gun . . . Hell, I don't know what I thought. But when I saw that radio and realized Trey must be a cop, I was shaking so hard I had to pull off the road. I didn't think about anything else all day, except how close I'd come to doing something stupid."

At another time, I might have congratulated myself for figuring that one out with so little to go on, but I wasn't feeling very cheerful. Whether the official time of death broadened to include several hours—wiping out a number of alibis—didn't matter much in Peter's case. If finding out Trey was a cop had scared him off buying a gun, there wasn't much doubt it would have discouraged him from committing two murders.

Almost absently, I said, "Something you should be grateful for, I'd say."

"Yeah, tell me about it."

Peter continued on into the house, and I went through the solarium and out to the veranda, which was still warm in the late afternoon sunshine. It didn't surprise me much that Jason was there. He was sitting on one of the lounges with a big sketch pad on his knees, occupying his time and—probably—trying to take his mind off the troubles besetting our family.

Choo had come out with me, and as I sat down on a chair across from Jason's, he leaped up on the foot of the lounge and spoke to my brother.

"Pose for me, Choo," Jason instructed, looking over his sketch pad at my cat.

The experts can say all they want about our tendency to humanize our pets, and they can argue till hell freezes over that cats don't understand English, but they will never convince me. I wasn't at all surprised that Choo made himself comfortable, lifted his chin, half closed his eyes, and went perfectly still as he responded to Jason's request. He's a born ham and loves having his picture taken.

There is a framed sketch of a kittenish Choo in my loft, and he's been known to take visitors to see it.

"Good, that's good," Jason muttered, sketching rapidly. "Oriental inscrutability."

"What're you doing?" I asked.

"A montage," he replied. "I've been working on it all day. I thought about calling it One Man's Family, but Faces of Murder seems more appropriate for this weekend. Is the questioning over?"

"I expect so, by now, at least for today. Winslow's going to be frustrated when he finds out Grace wore earplugs to bed because Innis snored."

Jason looked over his sketch pad at me, his expres-

sion thoughtful. "I imagine that means something," he
commented, "but for the life of me I don't know what."

I had to laugh, albeit faintly. "Sorry. It appears that
Cain went to Innis's room late last night and had a hell
of an argument with him. Alexander overheard, but not
enough to provide Winslow with the motive he so desperately needs. Cain and Maddy are holding fast, so
Winslow had the bright idea of asking Grace what *she*
had overheard. She told me years ago that she always
wore earplugs to bed because Innis snored—so I doubt
very much if she heard anything."

Jason frowned. "Am I correct in assuming that the
good captain has fixed his sights on one suspect?"

"Yeah, damn it. Cain."

My brother's handsome features tightened, but he
didn't look very surprised. "How strong is his case?"

"Wauur."

"Sorry, Choo—half a minute."

I watched my brother complete his sketch of Choo,
and waited until he announced he was done, then
watched my cat work busily on perfecting his forepaws.

"Well?" Jason demanded.

"Hell, I don't know. Unless the lab comes up with
evidence, it's all circumstantial. He has a witness who
can place Cain in Innis's room eight or nine hours before the murder and overheard him threatening to kill
Innis. He has a cuff link apparently dropped in the room
last night to verify Cain's presence. He has the fact that
Cain was bartending when Lawrence died, with the
perfect opportunity of poisoning a drink."

I sighed. "Now Winslow's hot on the trail of a motive. Apparently, Alexander overheard enough to be
fairly sure Cain was furious because of something Innis

had done to Maddy. But Cain and Maddy aren't saying what that might be.''

Jason frowned at me. ''I thought the police didn't have to prove motive.''

''No, but with a circumstantial case, a strong motive might make all the difference. I'm worried, Jase. Winslow's sure Cain is guilty, and he's not very willing to listen to any other possibility.''

''Have you offered him one?''

''I'm open to suggestions.''

Jason sketched idly for a moment, then lowered his knees (jogging Choo, who grumbled), and studied me. ''Back away, Lanie,'' he said.

''What?''

''You're too close. The only thing you can think about is the danger to Cain, and that's blocking all your instincts. If you have any hope of figuring out what really happened, you have to be as detached as you were this morning. Look at it as a puzzle with only one logical solution—nothing more.''

Good advice. I just wasn't sure I could take it.

''Let me see the sketch,'' I said, stalling for time.

He leaned forward and handed it over, a lifted eyebrow informing me that he knew a distraction when he saw one.

As I've told you, my brother is a gifted artist. He's uncanny at capturing personality with a few lines and a little shading. The charcoal sketches on the page were indicative of his talent. He'd put nearly everybody in: Trey, all the family, Alexander and several of the staff, Robin—the girl who'd had lunch with us the previous day—even Winslow and a couple of his men. And, of course, Choo.

"Do I really look so much like Mother?" I asked uneasily, surprised at the similarity of our features.

"Yes. And, like Mother, you'll age well. In case you were worried about that."

I eyed him. "You're a warlock." Then I suddenly realized. "Hey—you sketched me. You've never sketched me before."

"Mmmm. If you can spare the time in the next week or two, I'd like you to sit for me."

He really was uncanny. Thoughtfully, I said, "Okay, maybe it shows somehow that I'm in love; we all know I couldn't hide my feelings if I put a paper bag over my head. But you told me I'd have to *admit* it to the man I loved before you'd paint me; what makes you so sure I've told Trey?"

Jason smiled slightly. "It shows on him."

Drawing a deep breath, I said, "If you're not careful, somebody'll burn you at the stake."

"In this day and age? I'd probably get my own talk show."

He had a point. I returned my attention to his sketch, noting idly how strong a genetic trait could be between parents and their children. Peter owed much of his beauty to Innis, and his hadn't yet been spoiled. But like Dorian Gray, Innis could have used a painting walled up somewhere becoming loathsome, because what must have been beauty in his youth had not only aged, it had been distorted by all the unpleasant aspects of his character.

Yuk.

Wanda was going to look just like Kerry when she grew up, except for the premature graying of her hair inherited from Baxter. Vanessa resembled Adam. And

I couldn't really deny how much I looked like Mother, even though it was unnerving.

Something was nagging at me as I looked at the sketch, but I didn't know what it was. I kept studying the faces, half listening for my subconscious to tell me what the hell it was I was supposed to know. No luck, though. I thought I might be trying too hard, so I gave up for the time being.

"You cheated," I remarked, handing the sketch pad back to my brother. "You're not there."

"This is from my perspective, so I obviously don't belong," he said calmly. "Now—are we ready to talk about the real issue here?"

"What issue?"

"You. And the fact that you're wallowing in helplessness."

I glared at him. "I am not."

"Sure you are. Lanie, we both know how you feel about our legal system. You're not real confident that innocent people are always judged innocent. So you've got yourself half convinced that Cain will end up paying the price for murder. And it's got you scared to death."

"Aren't you scared?" I demanded.

"Worried, yes. But I'm putting my money on you."

"Don't do that. I don't have a clue, Jase, really."

"That's because you're not looking at the puzzle. Lanie, Cain isn't guilty. We both know that. So—who is? Stop trying to pick at the so-called evidence against Cain and look at the facts. Just the facts, ma'am."

He did a lousy Jack Webb impression. I said, "It's not as easy as that."

"Why? It's what you did during the Townsend investigation, isn't it?"

"I didn't know any of them—"

"No, you didn't. But you still managed to piece together the facts until everything fit. That's what you have to do here. The first fact is that you *do* know all of us. The second fact is—you find things. So find the truth, and find the evidence to support that truth."

"Have you been talking to Trey?" I asked wryly.

Jason smiled. "Of all of us, Lanie, including Trey and Winslow, you have the best chance of figuring it out. Unlike Trey and Winslow, you know us very well; unlike me or anyone else in the family, you know how to put together a puzzle made up of a lot of disparate pieces. In case you didn't know, you're very good at that."

I shook my head. "Jase, there's too much pressure. I feel like I'm being pushed and prodded and rushed along. Like I'm running out of time. This is my *family*, and I can't help feeling about them. All I can think about is what kind of reason Cain might have had—"

Jason shook his head sharply. "No, that doesn't matter. He didn't do it, so his motives aren't important. The only important motives are the ones of the murderer. Cross Cain off your list. Cross off all of us you know didn't do it. Then start with what's left."

I lifted my hands helplessly. "But there are so few facts. We're not even positive Innis was killed between nine and nine-thirty; that's just an estimate and one I doubt is going to hold up. The medical examiner may be cagey—they mostly are—and say it was between eight and ten. Half an hour either way of the original estimate, and almost anybody could have done it. Peter could have, or Grace. Even Mother or Adam. Hell, even you could have."

Jason rose to his feet, holding his sketch pad. "That's

why you have to depend on your own knowledge and intuition. Which of us do you *know,* in your gut, didn't do it? That's your first question. Go from there.''

I watched my brother go into the house, my thoughts chasing their own tails in a helpless kind of way that was maddening. As Jason had observed, my detachment of the morning had fled. Just as I'd feared from the start, someone I loved could end up being convicted of murder, and the idea was so frightening and painful I was having a difficult time getting past it.

If the medical examiner discovered some exotic poison in Lawrence (which required scientific knowledge to produce, say, or was found only growing under green elm trees in South America), or the forensic team discovered that the hair stuck in the blood on the newspaper Innis had dropped wasn't Choo's at all, but actually belonged to the murderer (who had, for some insane reason, draped the paper over his head after killing Innis), well, that would at least provide a few facts to get my teeth into.

Fat chance.

The problem was—there weren't many absolute facts of any kind surfacing in this investigation. Too many fingerprints on one murder weapon, and none on the other. One death literally before our eyes, and the other occurring in silence and secret. One victim who was totally inoffensive, and another who'd been lucky to live as long as he did.

It had to make sense. *Somehow,* it had to.

Innis had been asking for it, and almost any of the family could have been—at least momentarily—willing to oblige him. He'd treated his wife and son like dirt, and insulted or grossly offended everyone else. He hadn't been in the house two days before he'd screwed the daughter of his host (sorry for the crudity, but knowing Innis and remembering what Vanessa had said, that's just what they'd done).

So who could be surprised at finding him with his head bashed in? Nobody, that's who.

Something flickered in the back of my mind then, but I was in no state to pounce on it. I was feeling miserable, depressed, and totally confused. How in hell was I supposed to solve a murder when I couldn't even think straight?

Damn, damn, *damn*.

I don't know how long I sat there, but the air was getting chilly and the light was the bloodred of sunset when I became aware of my surroundings again.

"Lane?"

I blinked, focusing on Mother as she came toward me across the veranda. She was very pale, and I felt a little chill spread out from my bones. Something had happened, I was sure of it. She sat down on the lounge Jason had abandoned, automatically stroking Choo as she looked at me.

"What's happened?" I asked slowly.

She cleared her throat, the way someone does when something very difficult has to be said. "I've just talked to Grace. Captain Winslow asked her about Cain's argument with Innis, and she told him she didn't hear it because of the earplugs she'd worn to bed."

Nodding, I said, "I thought she wouldn't be able to say anything about the fight. So?"

"Right after that, just a few minutes ago, Grace came to me." Mother's lips firmed, and a combination of pain and anger tightened her features. "If she'd come to me when she first found out, much of this could have been avoided. I would certainly have refused to admit Innis to this house.''

''What did she tell you?''

''What Innis confessed to her nearly ten years ago. I don't know why he told her—perhaps because he was afraid someone else would, or because he was a sadist.'' She sighed. ''He took a business trip out West during the winter about ten years ago, and made a point of visiting Cain's ranch for the first time. Cain was away on a stock buying trip, so Maddy was in the house alone. Innis's reasoning—according to Grace—was that she was behaving seductively. I think we both know what that's worth. He raped her, Lane.''

NINE

"OH, GOD," I muttered, sickened.

Mother looked a bit sick herself. "Cain would have killed him if Maddy had told him what happened. I'm sure she never did. But I think he knows now. I think Innis somehow gave himself away this weekend—and that was what the fight was about."

Quite suddenly, I remembered Cain's white face at lunch the day before. I had merely assumed Innis was running true to form and insulting everyone at that end of the table. Maybe he was. Or maybe, in his malicious recklessness, he had said something, betrayed some knowledge of the ranch (Innis had never been an invited guest, and I was reasonably sure he'd never gone back there after raping Maddy).

Cain was smart, and he was quick at picking up details. He could have realized Innis had been to the ranch, maybe inside the house—and that Maddy hadn't told him, for some reason. Knowing Innis, he would have suspected the worst. And he wouldn't have wasted any time in asking Maddy.

What had they done after lunch? I couldn't remember. But I didn't think I'd seen them again until we all

met for drinks. Had they spent all that time alone? Had
it taken all that time for Maddy to confess—or for her
to calm my uncle?

I still didn't believe Cain had killed Innis. But I now
knew he had a hell of a motive for the murder. A jury
would probably be sympathetic, I thought. But this was
clearly a case of premeditated murder, and sympathy
might not stop them from returning a guilty verdict.

If Cain were arrested.

And all because Innis was one of those people Trey
had referred to: born without a conscience.

"How could Grace stay with him?" I asked helplessly.

"I don't know. She was crazy about him when they
were first married. And he was different then, when he
was younger, not so cruel to the people around him.
Oh, he was unfaithful to her, but she seems convinced—by him, no doubt—that he couldn't fight his
own nature. It was just a series of female bodies to him,
and since he never left her, I suppose she persuaded
herself that he loved her."

I thought about Maddy, sweet, gentle Maddy—and if
Innis had been standing in front of me right then I
could have killed him without a moment's hesitation.
God*damn* the bastard for tearing my family apart!

"Lane, you do see what this means? From what I
understand, Captain Winslow is convinced Cain is
guilty. Grace didn't tell him what she knows, but if he
asks her directly she will—she feels she has to. That
gives Cain a very strong reason to have killed Innis."

Automatically, I said, "If he'd intended to kill Innis,
he would have done it last night when they were fighting, you know that."

"I know. But does Captain Winslow believe it?"

"I—no, I don't think so. Mother, why are you telling me all this?" Right then, it felt like an overwhelming burden, that knowledge of secret crimes. I didn't want it.

Tilting her head slightly and wearing a very serious expression, my mother said, "Someone has to find the truth. That is what you do, isn't it?"

"I find *things*. Things that are lost. People that are lost."

"Isn't a murderer lost?"

For a moment, I didn't know how to answer that. In one sense, you could say a murderer was lost. Lost to whatever controls keep the rest of us from killing, I suppose. Still, that wasn't a search I'd chosen for my career.

Not that it mattered. If nothing else, I'd at least accepted the responsibility of doing whatever I could to get at the truth. Whatever I could . . . God, I felt so helpless. Jason had been right; I was wallowing in that helplessness.

"Mother, I'm going to do everything I can to figure out what happened. But I don't know if that'll be enough. All I can do is try."

"That's all anyone expects you to do." She hesitated, then seemed to brace herself in order to go on. "Do you know why you find things?"

Irritably, I said, "Why does everyone always ask me that? I find things because I've got some weird radar inside me to point me in the right direction."

"Let me put it another way. Do you know why you look for lost things?"

"Because they're lost. It's getting cold out here—why don't we go inside?"

"Lane . . ." She hesitated again, then sighed. "All

that's happened this weekend has made me realize something. Old hurts can't be allowed to fester until they're unbearable—and each of us has to settle with our past.''

''I don't want to have this conversation,'' I said, feeling suddenly panicked. As if, like Choo, I smelled blood.

''Why? Because it's easier to blame me for your father leaving?''

''Mother, there have been two murders in this house. I think that takes precedence over—''

''No. It doesn't. You and I have acted like strangers for twenty years, and it's time we stopped.''

''We're different, Mother,'' I said tightly. ''We don't agree on much.''

''That's just an excuse. And any excuse would have been fine, wouldn't it? Any excuse. As long as it wasn't the real reason. You told me that only once, out loud. When you were eleven. When Christmas and your birthday had passed without even a card from your father. You said it was my fault that he left. And you still believe that.''

I might have denied it, just the way I'd denied it to myself for twenty years, but I couldn't. Not anymore. Not then.

More than anything else, that weekend had made me conscious of ties. Ties of blood. Ties of emotion. My stiffness with Mother. The panic I'd felt whenever a conversation had skated dangerously close to the subject of my father.

It's difficult to accept the fact that your own father was a louse. For an adoring daughter of ten, coping with the pain of being abandoned, it had been impossible.

I could remember haunting the mailbox, hovering near the phone. Crying myself to sleep. I had blamed Mother because it had been unbearable to blame myself—and because I couldn't bring myself to blame him.

But Mother hadn't kept him away from us for more than twenty years. He could have called, written—something. Whatever hurt she'd felt, Mother wouldn't have denied any man the right to see his own children. If he'd wanted to.

And it wasn't as if he hadn't been able to find us. Jase and I had remained here, in Dad's family home, until we were in college. He could have found us.

If he'd wanted to.

God, we carry our emotional baggage for so long . . .

"Why did he leave?" I heard a lost note in my voice that was alien—yet so terribly familiar, because it belonged to the child I had once been. "What did we do to make him leave us?"

Mother shook her head. "I asked myself that question for so many years. It was easy to accept your blame, because I blamed myself. If I'd been a better wife or mother, if I had given him whatever it was he obviously felt was lacking . . . Even now, I don't have the answer. He had a good job, a beautiful home, two wonderful children—and a wife who loved him. Somehow, it wasn't enough for him."

"You cried," I said. "When he called and said he wasn't coming back. I'd never seen you cry before."

"I was . . . devastated. I loved him so much. It was a long time before I could accept that he wasn't coming back." She sighed a bit raggedly. "And when I did . . . I was frantic to find what I'd lost. So I married, convincing myself I was in love again—and then ended it before he could. It became a pattern I was too blind to see.''

"What's different this time?" I asked slowly.

"Adam," she replied simply. "I love him. Really love him, the way I loved your father. Even more, I trust his love for me." She paused, then continued quietly. "Maybe that's why I can't go on accepting the blame for Daniel's leaving. *He* left, Lane. It wasn't your fault, or mine, or Jason's. We loved him. Walking away from that was his choice.''

"You . . . haven't heard from him since the divorce?"

"No. Not since that phone call. Lawyers handled everything, and since I refused alimony or child support and he wanted none of the possessions we had, there was no court battle.''

None of the possessions. Not even his children.

I had searched for him once, when I was in college. The trail hadn't taken me very far, and had dead-ended; I hadn't really known how to search, not then. Could I find him now? Probably, if he was still alive.

I didn't want to find him.

Suddenly, for the first time, I understood a few remarks Jason had made, and understood Mother's question about my reasons for looking for lost things. Until then, I really hadn't known why I had chosen my career, hadn't realized how much my father's abandonment had shaped me.

But it made sense. The one lost thing I had cared about was lost to me forever. Even if I found him, even if he stood in front of me, I'd never get my father back. So I searched for other people's lost things.

There was an ache deep inside me, an old ache, but despite that I felt suddenly calm. I was going to have to thrash out my feelings about Dad, I knew, but for now at least the anger at Mother was gone.

"I'm sorry," I said. Finally, after twenty years, I could say the words. And if they didn't erase the accusation I had made, they did begin to heal an old wound.

She smiled a bit hesitantly. "Me, too. For all the years I ran away from . . . everything. I guess I was no more ready to talk about it than you were."

There was a brief silence between us, a little self-conscious but more peaceful than anything we'd shared in years. Then I realized it was getting dark, and got slowly to my feet.

"Almost dinnertime. If any of us feels like eating."

Mother rose as well. "Alexander suggested a buffet, and no one objected. But most everyone is very tense."

"I know. Mother, I'll try to find out who killed Innis."

"I know you will." She hesitated, then shook her head a little. "Poor Lawrence. We've all but forgotten about him."

Conscious of a peculiar jolt, I stared at her. "Yes. We have, haven't we?"

WE *HAD* VIRTUALLY forgotten about Lawrence. Oh, we'd all been mentioning him, but we—meaning me, Trey, and Winslow in particular—had actually paid very little attention to his murder. Winslow had said his background and finances would be checked out, and everybody was concerned about how the poison had got into his glass, but as far as I could tell, none of us had really pondered the enigma of that first victim.

Since the moment it became apparent that the glasses could have been switched by accident, all of us had begun forgetting about poor Lawrence. Then, when Innis was killed so soon after, the first murder had become even less important except by comparison to the second (for instance, since Cain had been bartender, he *could* have poisoned Lawrence—so he could have committed both murders).

At first, all I had was a vague possibility, an idea of who but still baffled as to why. Snatches of conversation and thought flitted through my mind, disjointed and tangled.

If Innis had been the intended victim, motives were everywhere . . . Blood ties . . . Nobody was surprised when Innis was killed . . . The glasses could have been accidentally switched . . . Somebody had kicked Choo . . . Poison in the glass . . . How much we owe to genetics . . . That voice out in the garden—not Vanessa, no . . . Innis killed so soon, and a cop in the house . . . Why? It had to be desperation, nothing else made sense . . . The only time the family noticed poor Lawrence was when he died . . . Old hurts, festering . . . There wouldn't be a motive the cops could uncover, I was willing to bet that—not for both the murders . . . Because only one motive counted . . . So what was it? What had happened during this fairly normal—or at least routine—weekend to trigger a murder?

There must have been a trigger, because I doubted it had been planned beforehand. Trigger . . . a catalyst. A substance which caused a reaction without being consumed in that reaction. Something which, just by being, caused an explosion. What was it? *What?*

A puzzle . . . one logical solution. One missing piece.

What was different about this weekend? What new element had been introduced into the family?

All through dinner, I thought about it, eating automatically and taking blessedly little notice of just how tense most of my relatives were.

I do remember realizing that Peter was the only one who was really relaxed. Judging by the thoughtful expression in his eyes, he was clearly just beginning to contemplate the likely benefits of a life without Innis, and I didn't think anyone could blame him for being pleased.

I certainly didn't.

I also didn't say much during dinner, which is probably one reason Trey might have thought I was mad at him. As soon as we were finished, I suggested that we go up to our suite. He agreed, ignoring a muttered ribald comment from Vanessa.

To this day, I'm often sorry that I couldn't prove Vanessa a murderess.

Anyway, we went upstairs, and as soon as we were in the bedroom, Trey said, "Montana, I had to go along when Nick decided to spring that cuff link and the argument on you."

I have to admit, I wasn't really paying attention. "Hmmm? Oh, that. I know you did. I'm not mad about it, if that's what you think."

I wrestled my Reeboks off (for once, none of us had bothered to dress for dinner), and climbed up onto the bed, banking the pillows and making myself comfortable. Trey joined me, leaning back on one elbow near the foot of the bed so that we faced each other.

"You've got something, don't you?" he said slowly.

A cop's eyes. In the lamplight, they were more luminous than ever. Funny—I'd never noticed before how clean and clear that direct, searching look really was.

Forcing my mind back to the matter of murder, I

said, "An idea occurred to me. I think it's from an old mystery. 'A' wants to kill 'C', but kills 'B' first, to divert suspicion."

"Because he has no motive to kill 'B'?" Trey nodded. "Okay. And so?"

I'd spent the past hour mentally organizing my arguments, but I spoke slowly and carefully. "Suppose, just for the sake of argument, that what we have here is a variation of that. 'A' wants to kill 'B'—and does—then kills 'C' in order to divert suspicion. Not because 'A' has no motive to kill 'C', but because *everyone* has a motive."

"Lawrence," Trey murmured, his eyes narrowing thoughtfully.

"He was the one who died first. But it seemed so obvious, didn't it? Poor Lawrence died after mistakenly drinking from Innis's glass. It was so obvious that none of us even considered that the glasses just as easily could have been deliberately switched. Identical glasses, a confusion of fingerprints, the proximity of both men—and the undeniable fact that Innis was the one with enemies—made the entire situation seem so clear that it was easy to start forgetting about Lawrence.

"It was a very neat little murder. There was no conflict with times or alibis; all the suspects could have done it. The poison was readily available, easily found, and any of us could have. Each of the switched glasses was virtually guaranteed to have more than one set of fingerprints on it, especially if they were switched *before* the poison was added—after Innis, Vanessa, and Cain had all handled Innis's glass."

"That could have been pure luck," Trey speculated. "Innis and Lawrence both drank scotch, which Cain always poured into identical glasses. The killer could have been waiting to poison Lawrence, noticed that Innis had set his drink down on the table and then picked up Lawrence's by mistake, and decided the timing was perfect.''

I nodded. ''That's logical. Having our attention turn toward Innis might have been a spur-of-the-moment plan that formed only after Innis picked up Lawrence's glass by mistake. So, the killer drops poison into the glass Innis *had* been drinking from, Lawrence drinks the poison—and dies. Now. We help the killer build the deception when we see the glasses could have been switched and decide almost immediately that Innis was the intended target. Even before the autopsy and the forensic evidence are in, the focus of the investigation shifts to who wanted to kill Innis. We stop looking for one motive—the one that caused Lawrence's death—and concentrate on sorting through all the painfully obvious motives surrounding Innis.

''Then, when Innis is killed just over twelve hours later, we're even more sure.''

''And Lawrence's death fades further into the background,'' Trey said. ''Goddamn it, one of the basic questions to ask is, who was killed. It's an obvious question, but easily overlooked. I shouldn't have overlooked it.''

Sighing, I said, ''Well, try to keep in mind that Lawrence only died last night; none of us has had time to sort through everything. Besides, if it'll make you feel any better, it was partly my fault.''

Trey looked surprised. ''Yours? How?''

''I kept dragging all my doubts and fears into the situation, clouding all the questions we *should* have asked with a lot of totally unnecessary junk.''

"I wouldn't call it junk," he murmured, smiling faintly.

"Whatever. The point is, I made it harder on you than it needed to be. Sorry."

"I'll forgive you. If, that is, you've figured out who our murderer is."

Cautiously, I said, "Well, I think I have. But I can't quite get a fix on the motive. That's the only thing that doesn't make sense to me. I thought—very fleetingly— right at the beginning that the family took so little notice of Lawrence that none of us could have *felt* enough about him to be driven to kill him. But if we assume Lawrence was the intended target of the first murder, then somebody had to feel strongly enough about his life to want to end it. And, as far as I could see, there was only one person who could fit the bill."

"Emily."

"Yeah. She was sitting right beside him that night, and could have very easily dropped poison into his glass without any of us noticing. And she was at no time suspected of killing Innis; she was sedated this morning, we all knew that. Mother said so at breakfast. And—what I consider the clincher—the haste of Innis's murder.

"Think about that for a minute. Barring Vanessa, nobody in this house is stupid. There was a murder investigation under way. We were all under suspicion. There was a homicide detective in the house. And yet, only a few hours later, Innis is murdered. Now, the *only* logical reason anyone could have had to take such an insane chance would be the desperate need to make damned sure our attention was focused on Innis—and away from Lawrence."

"It makes sense to me." Trey frowned slightly. "So,

she palmed her sedatives this morning, and when Peter drew Grace out of the room, she took the opportunity to slip across the hall and kill him. If Choo somehow got into the room at the same time . . . She's afraid of cats, isn't she?"

I wasn't surprised he'd noticed; he was a cop and a cat person, and neither one would have missed it. "A borderline phobia, I think. And Choo felt it, the way cats do. He wouldn't have gone to her if she called, especially with the smell of blood in the room. She didn't know how much time she had before Grace came back, and she certainly couldn't afford to just open the door and let Choo find his own way out. She wanted to delay discovery of the body for as long as possible. Between television and movies, most everybody knows the longer a person's been dead, the harder it is to pinpoint the time of death."

I shrugged. "So—she had to get Choo out of there. She kicked him or hit him with something, he got blood on his fur trying to get away from her and then ran out. She slipped back into her room, took the sedatives, and appeared to be sleeping deeply by the time Grace returned. No one suspected her, especially since she's been so obviously tanked to the gills with sedatives and in shock over Lawrence's death."

"A convincing act," Trey noted.

"Yeah. I should have guessed, though. I mean, I knew she was a hypocrite, and they always act. She smiled all the time, but the only words out of her mouth were sweet criticisms and feigned affection. Everybody was *dear* to her—even Choo, for God's sake."

"Which brings us to the question of motive. And proof."

I realized I was chewing on my thumbnail, and made

myself stop. "Well, as to proof—there isn't any. I'll bet she never touched the glass. Nobody saw her go into or out of Innis's room. And even if the forensic team found a sliver of her toenail polish in there, it could be easily explained—just like fingerprints on the doorknob or on anything else, barring the murder weapon. Maybe if we'd given her a blood test earlier today, we could have proven she'd taken the sedatives later than was believed, but even if we had, it would only prove she *could* have walked across the hall and bashed Innis, not that she did."

Trey nodded. "Agreed. So let's concentrate on motive. Maybe if we know why she did it . . ."

"We might get a confession?" I brooded about that. "Possible, I guess. But she killed two men in a little more than twelve hours, and I can't see that she's lost her nerve or her head so far. Still, it seems to be the only shot we have."

"So what do you think? Money? Inheritance, insurance policy, something like that?"

Like most good cops, Trey quite naturally considered monetary gain the most likely reason. Good cops believe that because it's the sole motive for a large number of murders. But, in this case, I couldn't buy it.

There was something I was trying to bring into focus, a nagging feeling that I'd overlooked something. Something I'd seen or heard . . .

"I don't think so," I said slowly. "Trey, I don't think Emily planned to murder her husband here. When they first arrived, I mean. I think something happened on Friday, or yesterday, that drove her to do it."

"Intuition?"

"Maybe. Or maybe years of knowing them. I really believe that Emily, for all her pretentious mannerisms and hypocritical shows of affection, honestly loved Lawrence. If she *did* kill him, it had to be because something had changed—after they arrived here. He must have hurt her or betrayed her in some awful way she simply couldn't forgive. Instead of divorcing him, she killed him."

Trey didn't discount that motive as irrational; in police work, he'd no doubt seen even thinner reasons for one human being to murder another. Instead, he asked direct questions that made me think.

"What could he have done? They didn't leave the house or grounds. There was no obvious fight between them—the opposite, in fact, since she clung to him all the time. He didn't get a phone call or a message, or have a visitor that we know of. Did he suddenly go berserk and hit her? No visible bruise. Did he betray her by lusting after one of the other women in the house? There was no sign of that. What did he do, Montana?"

Frustrated, I said, "Maybe what he did wasn't visible to us. Maybe we just didn't see it."

"We must have," Trey countered calmly. "Otherwise, we won't be able to figure this out."

I couldn't help but grin at him. "Now, that's a logical thought."

He grinned back, then considered the matter for several minutes in silence. "Okay," he said reflectively, "let's think about what we *did* see. According to you, this weekend was pretty normal—other than the murders, of course. Innis was a bit nastier than usual, you said, but I didn't see him attack either Emily or Lawrence. Did you?"

"No. He usually ignored them, so that hadn't changed."

"No help there, then."

I closed my eyes for a minute, but that didn't help. I opened them and stared at Trey. "I can't think of a thing, damn it."

"There must have been something. You know your family. What was different? What happened that was unusual from most of the gatherings in this house? Was something missing? Something added? When did things change?"

When the answer first occurred to me, I couldn't connect it to anything. But then something my mother had said rang in my mind, and I was barely aware of saying it out loud.

"Old hurts. Festering."

"What old hurts? Whose?"

"Wait right here—I'll be back in a minute." I didn't give him a chance to respond, but scrambled off the bed and raced out of the room.

It was still fairly early in the evening, but I lucked out in finding Jason on the way to his room rather than downstairs with the others. I was also lucky in that he was carrying his sketch pad.

"Jase, can I borrow that sketch for a while? The montage? I want to show it to Trey."

"Sure," Jason answered, handing over the sketch pad. "But why? Hey, don't tell me you've figured it out so soon?"

"I don't know. Maybe. I want to get Trey's opinion, and there *still* isn't any evidence, but if I'm right about the motive, we may not need it. We may be able to shock her into confessing. I think."

"Her? Her, who?" He brightened. "Vanessa?"

"No, not Vanessa. Worse luck." (Yes, I know—both of us were terrible.)

"Then who?" he demanded. When I only lifted an eyebrow at him (a trick I learned from Mr. Spock), he sputtered, "Lanie, don't you dare walk off without telling me!"

Relenting, I said, "Emily."

He stared at me. "But—"

"Yeah, I know all the buts. And I'm curious to see if you can fight your way past them. Think about *why*, Jase. We'll compare notes in the morning."

I left him muttering, "My sketch. Something about my sketch," to the slightly peculiar landscape (an artist's conception of a flower blooming on Mars) in the hallway near the door to his suite, and returned to Trey.

Climbing back up onto the bed, I arranged myself as before and opened the sketch pad.

"Jason's?" Trey guessed.

"Uh huh. He was sketching out on the veranda this afternoon, working on a montage of all of us. Something was tapping away in the back of my mind, but I couldn't figure out what it was then. When you asked what was different . . ." My voice trailed off as I stared down at the sketch, my gaze shifting between two faces and my mind working frantically.

Finally, I handed the sketch pad to Trey. "Tell me if I'm imagining things."

"What am I looking for?" he asked, studying Jason's depictions of all of us.

"Something that doesn't belong. You asked me what was different about this weekend. There was something different. Someone. There was a stranger in the house. And I think she was the catalyst."

Trey found the sketch. He also found the resemblance I had seen. I could see him turning it over in his mind, conjuring mental images to match the charcoal sketches. Then he looked up at me, silently waiting for my reasons.

"Emily couldn't have children," I said simply. "It was the tragedy of her life that she couldn't give her Larry a child. And, Trey—she and Lawrence had been married more than eighteen years."

"I don't believe in coincidence," he said, not disbelieving, but thoughtful.

"Neither do I. I think she came here—maybe followed him here—to confront him. I think it was her voice I heard in the garden yesterday crying out, 'How could you?' I had half noticed him in the garden earlier, then promptly forgot about it. But I'll bet that's where she confronted him. She told Wanda she was leaving, and then she doubled back, maybe because she'd seen him out there."

I drew a deep breath. "And I think Emily had seen the resemblance at lunch. Maybe she confronted him later—but I doubt it. She knew. It must have seemed like the ultimate betrayal. Not only had he been unfaithful to her, but another woman had produced his child. She couldn't stand that. So she killed him."

"It's a convincing motive," Trey said slowly. "And you've sold me. But how do we prove it? We could prove Robin was Lawrence's daughter, but that doesn't prove Emily killed because of it."

I'll admit here that I felt a certain amount of triumph at having (I hoped) figured it out. I even felt happier because, honestly speaking, if there had to be a killer in my family, and Vanessa couldn't be it, Emily would have been my next choice (yes, I know how that sounds, but I'm being honest here). But I realized then that the resolution of this mess wasn't likely to be totally painless.

I had liked Robin.

"We have to find her," I said. "She rented a horse at one of the local stables; that's a place to start. Someone might have seen her car, or got her full name. Her accent was more Alabama than Georgia, so she could be from there. Given Lawrence's salesman territory, she could be from anywhere in the Southeast. But we have to find her."

"And then?" Trey asked quietly.

He knew. We both knew.

"Surprise Emily," I said.

To GET THE wheels in motion as soon as possible, we went down to the library, and Trey called Winslow. (There were phone jacks in most of the suites, by the way, but no phone in our suite because I hadn't thought to tell Alexander we'd need one.)

Winslow was skeptical, I could tell that from Trey's side of the conversation. But, eventually, he was convinced that my theory was at least possible, and agreed to explore it. (As much as he wanted Cain for his murderer, he was too good a cop to discount another possibility without checking it out.) His men would visit all the stables in the area, and if anyone provided a description of Robin's car, the search would be on. If necessary, he'd contact the highway patrol in six states.

I didn't think that would be necessary. With my own father troubles, I found it easy to believe Robin would be somewhere nearby. After a confrontation such as they'd had, I would have found the nearest dark corner and huddled.

Which is what she had done. They found her in a small, cheap motel less than twenty miles away.

* * *

TREY TOLD ME that just after noon on Monday. He'd spent the morning in the library, remaining in touch with Winslow and getting the reports from the forensic team and M.E. in Atlanta. I had spent the morning talking with Mother (who I was counting on to make certain Emily wasn't sedated), Jason, and Adam, with the result that they'd agreed to find an excuse to gather the rest of the family in the parlor when the time came.

Oh—Jason had figured out who Robin was, and had been busy cussing himself for not having seen with his eyes what his fingers had known so clearly.

Anyway, as I said, Trey told me they'd found Robin. I had gone into the library to find out what was happening—and the final puzzle piece dropped into place.

"Robin's in shock, naturally," Trey said in the dispassionate voice that had once fooled me. "She's willing to help us. She blames herself for what happened."

Sitting on the corner of the desk, I sighed. "I hope her mother has sense enough to get the poor kid in therapy as soon as possible."

Trey leaned back in the chair and looked at me wryly. "I think her mother will need therapy as well. Montana, Lawrence was a bigamist."

I know my mouth dropped open. I felt it. "What?"

"You heard me. According to Robin, he married her mother just about eighteen years ago. They have a home about a hundred miles from the house he shared with Emily. And he's maintained both households all these years. For all we know, he may have had more than two wives."

After a moment, I said, "Isn't it ironic. Here's Innis, who can't keep his pants zipped, and whose wife timidly puts up with his chronic cheating for years; here's Lawrence, who everybody thinks is the soul of devotion and who is so mild he's practically invisible; and both of them are murdered because *Lawrence* fathers a child by another woman.''

Trey nodded, then said, ''We have at least an hour before Nick gets here with Robin. Maybe now's a good time for you to talk to Cain and Maddy. I know it hurt you when they shut you out as soon as the investigation started.''

I hesitated, then shrugged. ''I don't think it's something we can talk about. I can't apologize to them; if Cain had turned out to be guilty and I'd found something to prove it, I would have given it to you and Winslow. Eventually. You were right. The truth had to come out.''

Looking at me intently, Trey said, ''Cain did have a motive, didn't he? A very strong one.''

''Yes, he had a motive. But I didn't find out what it was until I'd left you and Winslow in here yesterday.''

Trey didn't ask what the motive was. I knew he never would. Instead, he returned to the question of relationships.

''After the Townsend investigation, you . . . escaped . . . to Cain and Maddy in Wyoming. If you don't clear the air with them, you won't have that escape again, will you?''

It took me a moment to frame a reply, but I finally did. ''When you were a little boy, did you have a treehouse?''

Trey nodded slowly.

''A safe place. What happened to it?''

''It's probably still there. It just gradually vanished from my life. I outgrew it, I suppose.''

''It took me a little longer to outgrow mine,'' I told him. ''My treehouse, my safe place, was a lonely ranch in Wyoming. It's still there. I'd probably still be welcome if I ran back there, even after all this. But I've finally outgrown it. I don't need it anymore.''

He nodded again, accepting that.

I got down from my perch and flexed my shoulders absently. I wasn't particularly looking forward to Robin's arrival and the scene I was counting on to follow. ''I would like to talk to Maddy about something else, though, before everything hits the fan.''

Trey waited until I was almost to the door, then said, ''By the way, the M.E. has answered your questions about why Lawrence gulped down poison and died so quietly. First, it was likely his sense of taste was off, because he was apparently in the recovering stages of a bad cold. And second, the poison was a mixture of a number of the chemicals we found in the storage room. The M.E. believes he felt very little pain, if any. The combination of chemicals acted to shut down his nervous system very quickly. His heart stopped.''

''Was there any forensic evidence?'' I asked. ''To point to anybody in particular, I mean.''

''The full prints on the glass belonged to Innis—and Cain. The partials look like Vanessa and Lawrence. There were no prints on the figurine. The hairs sticking to the newspaper belonged to Choo, and there were a few more in the room.'' Trey smiled slightly. ''No sliver of toenail polish. Nor anything else helpful. If you hadn't figured it out, Cain would have been arrested.''

''We don't have a confession yet,'' I reminded him.

''We'll get one.''

Since I was also pretty sure we would, I nodded and left him alone in the library. He'd wait there for Winslow's call telling us to make sure everybody was in the front parlor and ready for the surprise we'd planned.

I didn't much like any of it, but that hardly mattered. Anyway, my mind was on another painful subject. I found Maddy in the solarium, thankfully alone.

"Can we talk?" I asked directly.

She was sitting in a fan chair that gleamed in a shaft of sunlight, and she gleamed too. But her eyes were wary. "Of course, Lane."

I had no business doing it, but as soon as I sat down in a matching fan chair across from hers, I said, "Don't worry about Cain. He won't be arrested."

"He didn't kill either of them," she said.

"I know." Again, I shouldn't have done it—from the police viewpoint, at any rate—but I told her quietly about Emily and why she had done it.

Maddy was certainly relieved that Cain was no longer a suspect, and she showed a certain amount of sympathy for Emily, which surprised me. "I can understand how that could have shattered her, Lane. For a woman who wants children, it isn't easy to accept being barren. To see a child that should have been hers and know without a doubt that her husband had betrayed her must have been devastating."

After a moment, I said, "Did you and Cain want kids? You've never said."

She shook her head slightly. "For the first years of our marriage, there was no room between us for a child; we were completely wrapped up in each other. Then you and Jason started coming to us every summer and"—she smiled—"we had all the benefits of being parents with virtually none of the drawbacks or frustrations."

"I don't think I could handle it even part-time," I confessed a bit ruefully.

"You may decide otherwise one day. Or you may

prefer not to be a parent. No law says you have to.''
She looked at me steadily. ''But why don't you say
whatever it is you came out here to say, Lane?''

There was no easy way to say it, of course. And,
being me, I probably would have just blurted it out
anyway.

''Maddy . . . I know what Innis did to you. And I
just wanted to say . . . I'm so sorry.''

She was very still, her face closed. ''What are you
talking about?''

So I told her, what Mother had told me and what I'd
surmised from Cain's behavior on Saturday. It was very
difficult for her to talk about, but she finally did—
probably because I was so upset and Maddy's instinct
was always to soothe.

Anyway, I'd been pretty much on the mark about
Cain, and about Innis shooting off his mouth and giving
away more than he'd meant to during lunch on Saturday. He had said something about the ranch that he
couldn't have known unless he'd been there, and Cain
caught it. Maddy said that he brooded about it all day
on Saturday, but apparently wasn't able to ask her about
it. Then he saw her slap Innis out front.

''I didn't tell him then,'' she said. ''He asked about
the slap; I laughed and said it was just Innis being
himself and making an unwelcome pass. Cain knew
there was more to it, but he didn't press me on it. Not
until late that night, after Lawrence was killed and the
police were gone.''

''So . . . when he went to Innis's room, it was almost immediately after you told him what had happened years ago?''

She nodded. ''I know he came as close as he ever
has or ever will come to killing. But he didn't, Lane.

Innis at least had sense enough not to provoke him any further, and you know as well as I do that no matter how angry he was, Cain could never physically attack someone who hadn't struck him first.''

Yeah, I knew that.

Maddy looked at me steadily. ''It isn't just you he's closed out right now, Lane. It's everyone. I've had ten years to heal from what Innis did to me, but for Cain it's a new wound. And . . . his temper might have taken him too far this time. He was suspected of murder. He's dealing with that as well.''

''Maddy . . . you do understand why I worked with the police?''

She nodded. ''I also know it was a difficult decision for you. Cain will understand that, when he's had a little time. He gave you room when you needed it— now it's your turn.''

That made me feel a little better. But before I could enjoy the feeling, Trey came into the solarium to say that Winslow would arrive within ten minutes. So we had to gather the family in the front parlor and set the stage.

I'D RATHER NOT replay that scene exactly as it happened. It was a bit painful. Suffice it to say that when Winslow walked into the parlor with Robin, Emily went completely to pieces. She was raving when the two policewomen Winslow had borrowed from the state police managed to drag her from the room. And, by then, she'd confessed hysterically to killing Lawrence because he'd ''betrayed'' her, and Innis because she hated his guts even more than the rest of us had.

It emerged later that her pride had been wounded by Innis years before, and that had sown the seeds of hate.

She knew—being a lot more observant than I'd given her credit for—that he'd hit on the other women in the family (including Mother), but he had quite openly scorned Emily.

Another bit of irony: if he had made a pass at Emily, she might not have killed him.

Anyway.

When Emily had been dragged from the house, and a white and silent Robin had been more gently led away by another female cop, Winslow motioned me to join him in the entrance hall, where he gravely offered me his hand.

"You were right—Lane. I apologize for not taking you as seriously as I should have."

I shook hands with him. "Apology accepted, Nick. But the simple truth is, I got lucky."

"No, there was no simple truth. That's what *I* was looking for. There was a very complicated truth. Don't sell yourself short."

Then he shook hands with Trey and left, allowing the two of us to explain the whole story to those of my relatives who didn't know what the hell had happened. Trey made it very plain that I hadn't been prepared to believe any of my other relatives were guilty of murder (tactfully avoiding the subject of Vanessa), and that I was the one who had figured it all out.

I am not an overly modest woman, but I honestly felt it was more luck than anything else. A combination of things I'd seen and heard, and snippets of knowledge, had been tangled up inside my mind, and were untangled out of sheer desperation.

So I wasn't very comfortable with taking the credit and, as previously discussed with Trey, told Mother as soon as the exclamations and questions had ended that we were going to head back to Atlanta.

Mother said somewhat hesitantly that she and Adam were going to remain at the house for at least another month, and that they'd return again in the fall. Would we come back to the house for another weekend?

I thought we would.

Maddy gave me a hug. Cain didn't. I didn't think it was because he couldn't forgive me for siding with the police, but because he had, as Maddy had said, withdrawn emotionally from all of us—for the time being, at least. Maddy told Trey and me we'd have to come out to the ranch in the summer, when Atlanta became unbearably hot, and Trey told her he would enjoy that very much.

I think he knew that a part of me still needed that treehouse. And I guess he was right.

WHEN DO YOU finally grow up? Is it when you realize that, despite ties of blood, you're apart from your family and essentially alone? Is it when you can no longer gaze at loved ones with the unshadowed trust of your childhood? Is it when you take responsibility for your actions, even though those actions alter how others perceive you?

Is it when you fall in love, and admit for the first time that loving is a painful thing?

I suppose it's all of that. And more.

Not so bad, growing up. There's grief for the things you lost along the way, but life is full of prices to be paid. After all, the price we pay for childhood is the painful transition to adulthood.

From the back seat of the Mercedes and the prison of his carrier, Choo howled plaintively. I half turned in the seat to offer comfort, and caught Trey's luminous eyes.

I don't think I'd ever smiled at him so freely and honestly as I did then. I know he'd never smiled at me quite like he did that day.

Hey—growing up isn't bad at all. So what if I'd lost the unshadowed trust of childhood? I'd found something else, something I hadn't even been looking for.

The unshadowed trust between a man and a woman is something very special.

Very special, indeed.

ELLIOTT ROOSEVELT'S
DELIGHTFUL MYSTERY SERIES

MURDER IN THE ROSE GARDEN
70529-X/$4.95US/$5.95Can

MURDER IN THE OVAL OFFICE
70528-1/$4.50US/$5.50Can

MURDER AND THE FIRST LADY
69937-0/$4.50US/$5.50Can

THE HYDE PARK MURDER
70058-1/$4.50US/$5.50Can

MURDER AT HOBCAW BARONY
70021-2/$3.95US/$4.95Can

THE WHITE HOUSE PANTRY MURDER
70404-8/$3.95US/$4.95Can

MURDER AT THE PALACE
70405-6/$3.95 US/$4.95Can

America's Reigning
Whodunit Queen

Charlotte MacLeod
WRITING AS
Alisa Craig

Join the club in Lobelia Falls—

THE GRUB-AND-STAKERS MOVE A MOUNTAIN
70331-9/$2.95 US/$3.95 Can
THE GRUB-AND-STAKERS QUILT A BEE
70337-8/$3.50 US/$4.25 Can
THE GRUB-AND-STAKERS PINCH A POKE
75538-6/$2.95 US/$3.95 Can
THE GRUB-AND-STAKERS SPIN A YARN
75540-8/$3.50 US/$4.25 Can

And for more disarmingly charming mysteries—

THE TERRIBLE TIDE   70336-X/$3.50 US/$4.50 Can
A DISMAL THING TO DO   70338-6/$3.99 US/$4.99 Can
A PINT OF MURDER   70334-3/$3.50 US/$4.25 Can
TROUBLE IN THE BRASSES   75539-4/$3.50 US/$4.25 Can
MURDER GOES MUMMING   70335-1/$3.99 US/$4.99 Can